"Super smart, skewed, resonant and risky in the best possible ways, the fictions in Emily Greenberg's *Alternative Facts* explore the nexus where the problem called history collides with the problems called perspective, language, and narrativity. Stand back: an exhilarating, kinetic new talent is in the house."

—Lance Olsen,
author of *Absolute Away* and *My Red Heaven*

"The pleasures of reading Greenberg's stories are multitudinous and mind-boggling. There is wonder and exhilaration and hilarity, surprise—astonishment—at every turn, and such beautiful, persuasive strangeness throughout that one feels the world has gone atilt. These stories are disturbing, wildly thrilling, sometimes scary, *fun*. (Perhaps this is how it feels to ride a mechanical bull—if the bull had heart and was also very, very smart?) *Alternative Facts* offers a glorious simulacrum of life. All great fiction does this, of course—but Emily Greenberg has done double (triple, quadruple, octuple) duty by building her narratives upon what we think we already know. So buckle in and get ready to be thrown."

—Michelle Herman,
author of *Close-Up* and *Dog*

"Smart, funny, insightful. These stories make me want to find the mind that made them, burrow inside, and feast for days on a world that's strangely familiar but just skewed enough to show me where I come from. And possibly where I belong. A poised and exciting debut."

—John Haskell,
author of *The Complete Ballet* and *American Purgatorio*

"A fact is a thing done. A fiction is a thing made. And the fact is that Emily Greenberg has done made a fabulous fabrication of stereoptic and stereophonic stories collected in *Alternative Facts*. Greenberg constructs a contemporary Edith Hamiltonian mythology, concocting shared off-the-shelf cultural narratives out of holy holey whole cloth, steeping them in the frayed omnipresent miasmic memes of our everyday evidentiary electromagnetic stew. These stories are savvy, canny recombinant recipes of the possible, probable, and problematic times and spaces where we find ourselves residing and resigned. Brilliantly constructed deconstructions, these mad made things mix it up with the empirical imperative, tango and two-step backwards and in heels, only to spell out how easily our senses are foiled and fooled. *Alternative Facts* maps the facts of our resignation (sign and signifier) to a reality of now knowing unknowable knowns."

—Michael Martone,
author of *Plain Air: Sketches from Winesburg, Indiana* and *The Complete Writings of Art Smith, The Bird Boy of Fort Wayne, Edited by Michael Martone*

ALTERNATIVE FACTS

ALTERNATIVE FACTS

—— *STORIES* ——

EMILY GREENBERG

Kallisto Gaia Press
1801 E. 51st Street
Suite 365-246
Austin, TX 78723
info@kallistogaiapress.org

First edition January 2025

This is a work of fiction. Any references to historical events, real people, or real places are used fictitiously. Other names, characters, places, and events are products of the author's imagination, and any resemblance to actual events or places or persons, living or dead, is entirely coincidental.

Cover art and design: Raúl Lázaro
Book design: Raúl Lázaro
Author photo: Jason Wilbur

Library of Congress Cataloging-in-Publication Data is available.

ISBN: 978-1-952224-36-2 (paperback)

These stories have been previously published in slightly altered form: "Alternative Facts" in *Santa Monica Review*, "Black Box" in *Michigan Quarterly Review*, "Houston, We've Had a Problem" in *Chicago Quarterly Review* and *New Stories from the Midwest*, "Lost in the Desert of the Real" in the *Iowa Review*, "Tonight Show" in *J Journal*, and "From the Eyes of Travelers" in *Greensboro Review*.

To Andrew

In loving memory of my grandfather

CONTENTS

ALTERNATIVE FACTS

Maybe the two silver-haired, tuxedo-clad men were not really about to fight, Kellyanne thought, observing that no, they were not now puffing their concave, emphysemic chests and raising their voices like men did when they fought, nor were they folding their Mnuchin imitation eyeglasses and placing them on a nearby white-clothed cocktail table, shaved and moisturized cheeks reddening from the effort, carefully plucked first date eyebrows slanting, stumpy liver-spotted fingers jabbing the lavender-scented air, and maybe they were not stepping toward each other in that taunting, schoolyard-lunch-money-hungered way, sharp-eyed vultures circling a kill, curled fingers beckoning and half-parted lips mouthing *Come and get it*, and no, she was certainly not languishing in a forgotten corner at the inaugural ball on her fiftieth birthday, wilting like iced delivery flowers on the doorstep, waiting for the president and first lady to arrive, completely bored but feigning interest in her husband's small-stakes small talk with small-dick party donors, her husband who was not really her husband after all, which was fine, really and truly fine with her, not that anyone asked—not that anyone asked her anything about policy either, domestic or foreign, because, after all, she was only a glittering mouthpiece, a goldcast megaphone, a maw-gaping puppet—a snub which could only mean she was no longer senior counselor to the president, similar to how, when she first began managing the president's campaign, she was no longer the ex-campaign manager for the oily-haired Texas senator and had therefore never said all those awful things about the president, then her long shot opponent, things that were not true—that he had built his business on the backs of little guys, that he had conned customers—statements as false as the assertion that she was now inside the Walter E. Washington Convention Center, a 2.3 million square foot concrete-and-glass monstrosity whose perimeter was not currently lined with emptied garbage trucks—a barricade against basement-assembled bombs—or a wall of riot-ready cops blocking the furious protesters, those unwashed libtard riff-raff who would never see with their own delicate snowflake eyes her cherry-red gown cut off at the shoulder, which meant she was not really wearing it just like she had not worn the red, white, and blue cat-buttoned Gucci coat to the inauguration earlier, which of course she had not because no one could believe it, they could not believe their own peppermint-veined, stale bread-crusted eyes that she would desecrate such a solemn occasion with that gaudy getup, words the sniveling snowflake socialists-in-training muttered under their putrid, kale-inflected morning breath or posted on social media repeatedly, believing if they said or typed these words enough times with just the right mix of mock horror and ironic revulsion—*Oh no, she didn't, she DID NOT*—then it would become true, an event that had never happened, an event they could obliterate with their Pink Pearl erasers as she would erase the last eight years of a president who was never really the president, not for the reasons the current president and his followers believed but because no one was ever truly president, especially this new president, not because of his birthplace or skin color or the not-my-president jeers or because he had lost the popular vote, although obviously that fact was highly inconvenient, but because the presidency was not reducible to a single office or person, being instead a slow-burning network of popular resentments and untraceable power relations, an invisible industrially-polluted river coursing through them all so you had merely to dip your toes in the neon algal-bloom tides of history to catch the carcinogenic current and for the length of the ride the electrified chemical contaminants and sulfurous odors would flow through you and flow through him, making you all the president, even these two men who were not really about to fight and even her—yes, especially her—a fact she had not fully grasped until the inauguration, where she had not watched the president-elect approach the eagle-seal-stamped podium just before noon and recite the sacred oath while laying his little hand on the Lincoln Bible, his wife holding the Bible steady with her powder-blue Jackie-O gloves, French manicured fingers still freezing in the January cold, an action they'd practiced, not wanting to risk any mistakes, nor had she listened to him deliver one of the shortest inauguration speeches in history while pumping his tiny fists, his too-long tie waving, the rain falling, nor thought to herself, *He is whoever we tell him to be,* then looked out into the rain-drenched red-MAGA-hatted audience and thought, *He is whoever* they *tell him to be,* the hidden part of themselves they pretend doesn't exist, that slow-growing tumor, a thought that tickle-tortured her even more than watching

Forty-Three struggling to open a translucent poncho, bagging himself like week-old recycling as her husband squeezed her hand, his hairy palm warm and sweaty, always so sweaty, muttering over and over again as if hypnotized, *You did it, you did it, you made history*, a thoroughly superfluous statement given that history was always made, that it had never, in fact, existed outside its own making so that you could answer the old metaphysical thought experiment about the tree falling in the forest sans observers with ease—no, of course the fallen tree did not make a sound because the tree had not fallen if no one saw it, which might explain why she had not felt her chest swell with pride, her little rabbit's heart pitter-patter, hearing this long-awaited praise from her husband, a private praise no one else would hear, except she had also not felt her chest swell with pride when the president pledged before all to end American carnage in his tough-guy Queens accent, spitting as he said it, a no-nonsense New Yorker, describing a land of abandoned factories and rising crime, a land of forgotten men and women, a land that only became true when he spat it into existence, shaped it from the earth's red clay with scarred and bleeding palms and then breathed new life into the dormant heretical vision, that drowned blue-faced swimmer miraculously reviving on CPR kisses to cough up salty water, an ending as impossible as her standing here at the inaugural ball watching these two men who were not really about to fight, not listening to her husband laugh at a dead-eyed diplomat's joke that was not the least bit funny while not chewing on a sour martini olive, not stifling the self-splintering urge to scream that had developed after she had not received that mysterious package last week, the one confiscated so quickly she could forget it had even happened, so that when her youngest asked about the Secret Service detail, the silent looming men in matte black ties who called her Blueberry and smelled of Old Spice, it did not feel like a lie—really, it did not feel any different from just talking— to say there was no cause for alarm and that the strange men in dark suits with the funny earpieces were only helping Mommy manage her many admirers—those now setting limousines on fire in D.C. and chaining themselves to office buildings in downtown San Francisco—a natural consequence of her very important work, and no, these men did not really carry SIG-Sauer P229s, the package had never been sent, the threats never made, so that she was not now really putting her children at risk, which meant she was not such a bad mother after all either, as she had often said of her own mother, that Mama was not such a bad mother but merely an exhausted one, having stooped over an Atlantic City casino cash register for twenty-one years without a single complaint after her useless trucker husband walked out, her heels digging holes in the worn black pleather shoes, fingers stained black from unfolding creased bills, nostrils filled with cheap tobacco smoke, ears ringing from the constant clinking of quarters and the beeping machines, the whirring slots and the stuttering roulette wheel, fake smile dabbed on like dollar store makeup and always without a single complaint after he left her, not that anyone ever labeled him a bad father just like no one ever asked how her own husband, George, securities mergers and acquisitions lawyer, the one still joking with party donors at the inaugural ball, was securely merging and acquiring the demands of parenting and work, even as they asked her this over and over again, on the news and in fan mail and in person, their voices saturated with blame and judgment, those little raised questions at the end and the trailing off, forcing her to squint until the contradictory ripples resolved into a glass-smooth lake, a trick that was not difficult given that her blueberry blue eyes were not very good, meaning she was always squinting, as the president often did too, straight into the solar eclipse without sunglasses, watching *Fox & Friends* or *Shark Week*, the beady-eyed sharks grinning bloody murder, and squinting as she was now, she could not definitively say whether the two men were or were not really gearing up to fight after all, what with that haltingly hypnotic glare from the chandelier, the top tier Scotch she had swallowed, a smoky blaze down the throat, the very imprecision of human vision and perception more generally, the iris always shuttling in more or less light, the lens flipping the image to the retina like an overcooked pancake, the weary brain thermostatically readjusting the color balance, so that no one person ever saw the same thing, which meant, despite what her blueberry blue eyes were showing her, that the two men might actually not be gearing up to fight, freeing her from having to break them up, to manage the squabbling, snot-nosed children as she had all those months on the campaign trail and during the transition, crooning in her most honeyed, nurturing voice, *Hey, why don't we hold off on sending those tweets now because Mommy has a much nicer batch of tweets to send later, a wonderful chocolate cake with dark chocolate frosting but only after you eat your broccoli and use this teleprompter,* only of course there was no wonderful chocolate cake with dark chocolate frosting, no one had even remembered her big birthday, which was fine with her, really and truly fine, because it meant the birthday had not, in fact, happened and consequently she had not aged, her eyes were not weighted with purplish-blue bags, her cheeks not bloated with surreptitiously acquired collagen shots, this face that could not be half a century old because a woman over fifty was invisible—everyone knew that, even those who pretended otherwise—and an invisible woman could not be the public face of this administration, as she was, ergo she had not aged and was not a day older than when her husband first saw her on the glossy cover of a society magazine and asked Ann Coulter to introduce them, and if she was no older than this and they had not been introduced, then they had not attended Yankees games and vacationed in the Hamptons, nor had they married in an extravagant wedding at the Cathedral Basilica, where the wonderful chocolate cake with dark chocolate frosting was not cut in pieces to fit through the door, only there was no cake, there is never any cake, nor had they lived together in one of the president's gleaming Manhattan towers before he was president, nor had they ever even met the president before he was president, ergo they had turned back the clocks and made America great again, that wonderful slogan she had not said over and over again, four of the 1.2 million words she had not spoken on television as his campaign manager, a job she had not taken after her husband's warnings that she would be regarded as a second-rate captain on a doomed vessel, more Jack Sparrow than Blackbeard, the laughingstock of Washington—their words, he was careful to add, not his—he had not really said them, similar to how the president had not actually called Mexicans rapists or questioned the previous president's citizenship, a controversy she maintained he had instead put to rest by calling for the birth certificate in a manner not unlike how she had put the *Access Hollywood* tape controversy to rest, arguing that the president had not really done those things or said those things because he had said and done them so long ago that he was no longer the same person, not when the self was remade each and every day, so that it did not matter what he said or did in the past, not what dribbled from his mouth then but what was in his heart now, which could never be translated into words, which was why it was always best to speak English and only English here in these United States, learn it or leave it, words meaning one thing when they were surrounded by certain words and something else entirely when they were surrounded by certain other words, a word's meaning changing over time and changing depending on how you inflected it and changing when different mouths said it and even when the same mouth said it but at a different time or place, this being the entire history of literature as she understood it, all those volumes suffocating under library dust and mothballs, that you kept writing and talking, trying to say something that could never be expressed, thinking that if only you surrounded it with more words, words upon words upon words, words tumbling from your lips so quickly you had no idea what you were saying until you said it but maybe if you kept talking you could inch closer to it, could circle it as these two tuxedo-clad men were circling each other, spinning around like shining metal tops on a freshly Windexed glass patio table, stepping forward without ever getting closer, as if waiting for the right time to reach out and hold the thing, as if it were even possible to hold something without killing it, mount the butterfly without destroying its very butterfly-ness, the shimmering wing powders rubbed off on greedy fingers, the metal top clattering off the freshly Windexed glass patio table, but of course this was America so you could still call it a butterfly in the same way that an American could be whoever she said she was, which was the foundational lie, the brick-and-mortar lie, the lie Kellyanne must accept or else the whole structure would collapse, leaving her with nothing when the trick was to in-stead conceal the nothing and in concealing to create a something, to be a successful businessman even if your businesses all failed, to be a self-made billionaire even if you accepted your father's million dollar loan, to be a champion of the working class even if you ripped off the working class, so much smoke and mirrors you had to accept so the South Jersey daughter of a casino cashier and absent trucker could grow up to become senior counselor to the president, thus preserving the mythology of merit and Horatio Alger and pulling yourself up by the bootstraps when the truth was— and this she had learned quite early—that they would only accept her bootstraps if she first accepted their foundational American lie, and so she would, she had, she did, having long ago granted that truth was all in how she spun it, the new story she told herself each day, a lesson she had learned from eight subtropical summers picking blueberries in the swel-tering Jersey heat, eyes blinking away sweat, when she told herself that her toothpick arms did not really ache from hauling the blueberries, her skin did not really burn, and of course she did not really collapse into her hand-me-down bedsheets at night, in the crucifix-lined home smelling of mustard where she lived with her mother and grandmother and two aunts, in the town named after a corporation, the town haunted by the ghost of a little boy killed by a drunk driver while running after a muddy soccer ball, the town that told her she was useless, a statement that felt so true when she collapsed into the hand-me-down bedsheets, bone weary and dehydrated, rubbing her calves and dreaming of something better, only to run after that ball and reach that something better and unmask the town's lie, to graduate at the top of her high school class and attend college and then law school and make it as a pollster only to have to keep spinning herself new stories, that the male pollsters were not making deals on the freshly mowed golf course where they talked titties and twats and therefore couldn't invite her, that the congressmen had not really said those things to her or touched her in that way, and certainly this was no different from the stories she told about another man who had disappointed her, the very first man who had disappointed her, the absent trucker father who had not really abandoned their family but was instead working undercover as a spy or kidnapped by aliens or toiling away somewhere working hard and living simply, saving up greasy dollar after dollar so he could return one day like a winning lottery ticket, bestow on them another kind of life out of the blue, that life that she could not stop imagining in the endless blueberry fields, when she would not place her dented blueberry bucket on the ground and spin as fast as she could, around and around and around, the smooth angles of the field blurring until she was no longer sure what she was looking at, was no longer sure if she had ever known what she was looking at, until a tree branch faded into sky and cloud, the clouds morphing into her own father's grinning face as she imagined it must look—blueberry blue eyes like hers, square jawed, a little scar under the eye as a token of hard living—and her reality became something else too, a story where, as she often told news reporters these days, she was not the "victim of her circumstances" but the "product of her choices," one of which was to keep spinning, to spin so fast that she could decide her arms no longer ached from picking the sweetly sour blueberries—it was just the muscles growing, which was strength, the opposite of pain—to keep spinning no matter what punches anyone threw at her, verbally or physically, to never get caught on the sweat-stained boxing ring ropes but to bounce back, dodging and deflecting until the overmuscled man with cauliflower ears lost his balance, then redirecting the punch back at him, letting him knock himself out, convince him it was his idea in the first place, just like with the president and his tweets, because this was the thing the sniveling snowflake socialists-in-training had never grasped about the dialectic, that antithesis did not strengthen thesis, did not advance the argument closer to a common truth but merely revealed that the thesis as such had never existed, that it was all true or none of it was, and so she could only say that this is not what happened while she was not waiting for the president and first lady to arrive at the inaugural ball for their first dance: she did not leave her husband and the party donors, did not approach the men about to fight each other and ask what was wrong and implore them to use their words, not realizing her own words would be so misunderstood, that the men would hear only what dripped from her mouth and not see what was in her heart, her pitter-patter rabbit's heart, that one of the men would instead drunkenly slur to her that he did not listen to liars, that maybe the news media were all fools but *he* certainly wasn't, he would not listen to a word of what she said about how he should live his life, that was the truth, that was a fact, and so of course she did not really step forward and punch him in the face three times as one eyewitness later claimed in a Facebook post subsequently quoted in a *New York Daily News* story about the "alleged" incident.

***

BLACK BOX

noun

1. *Aviation*: a small machine that records information about an aircraft during flight, used to determine the cause of an accident.
2. *Military science*: also known as the "nuclear football," "the button," "the emergency satchel," a black leather briefcase containing the nuclear launch codes.
3. *Political science*: a theory of national and international politics in which the actions and relations of states and other groups are studied by looking at "input" pressures and actions and "output" policies, rather than at internal responses and calculations, including ideological or pragmatic considerations.
4. *Psychology*: in behaviorism, the view that mental processes are not legitimate objects of study, a perspective later hardened by the radical behaviorist B. F. Skinner, who excluded both inner experiential and physiological processes to focus only on external and observable behaviors, a practice largely rejected during the 1960s "cognitive revolution." According to cognitive science, one can crack open the black box of the mind, even the mind of the radical behaviorist himself.

A two-story wooden house in a railroad town by the river. On a hill overlooking the valley, the subject, B. F. Skinner, dreams of flight. He attempts to build a glider, stands on a Fairback beam and tries to make it tilt, practices levitation to test whether "faith will move mountains." With his brother, he feeds the pigeons in the garden overgrown with currant bushes and watches them take flight. Susquehanna is the City of Stairs, the smallest big city in America, a series of grandly named streets traversing hills several miles from the southern border of New York. Even as the hills rise toward the heavens, the valley's image sears his eyelids. He cannot unsee the coal-blackened shirts flapping

on clotheslines or the charred wooden houses, the carefully clipped news articles testifying to his mother's unre-
alized musical ambitions or the handwritten law diploma
his country-born father stores in a drawer and refuses
to frame. He cannot forget the chilled winter mornings
huddling over the vent for warmth or his mother reminding him not to play hide-and-seek among the gravestones
in the cemetery next door. His parents care greatly about
social conventions. *Do not do this, do not do that.* He is never
praised for doing the correct thing, for walking along
the footpath in the forest, holding his younger brother
Ebbie's sweaty palm and guiding them both home.

*

A cardboard packing box. As a child, the subject builds
himself a private reading room with a curtained entrance
and a shelf for books and pencils. Away from his parents'
prying eyes, he reads Verne, Swift, and Defoe. He types stories and poems on his father's typewriter and dreams of becoming a writer. Since his faith was insufficient to move
mountains, he instead renders the movement on the page.
Stone by stone. A better, more heavenly world. If he can
render the miracle on the page, maybe he can make it true.
He can fly, he can lift off the mountain and reach heaven.

*

An old heating stove. One day, the subject's limping grandmother throws open the door so he can feel the dry heat
and learn that hell is just around the corner. "This is what
happens to bad little boys who misbehave," she says. *Do not
do this, do not do that.* He is ten years old. The war in Europe

has just begun. His heart pounds mechanically like the chimes of a grandfather clock, like the Erie's short, shrill whistles waking him each morning. For months after feeding his brother's pigeons alcohol-soaked corn and lying about it, he cannot sleep, so much does he fear hell's eternal flames. He tosses and turns in his little bed while his brother sleeps soundly across the room, small hands folded across his chest. Ebbie has also told lies but about far more innocent matters. Not completing his homework. Stealing a chocolate bar from the store. Would a just God really burn a little boy forever for telling such harmless lies? The subject wants to live in a world where God rewards the good but does not punish the wicked because he does not believe any person truly *is* wicked, only that people sometimes *behave* wickedly. Can humans build such a world? A world where no one behaves wickedly because good behavior is rewarded?

*

A small shack the subject builds from red fence boards abandoned at the cemetery. There is nothing sacred about the cemetery now that he has stopped believing in God, now that he's decided people must build heaven themselves. "What will others think?" his parents ask, but he doesn't care what others will think. As the war in Europe rages on, he dreams of inventing a better world. From the blacksmith shop behind his house, he salvages car parts and oil-soaked oak planks to construct splintery slides and merry-go-rounds, creaky seesaws and steerable wagons. Improvising his inventions on the fly, he makes do with what he finds. A discarded water boiler converts into a potato-and-carrot-shooting steam cannon. A cigar box becomes a violin, a comb a kazoo, a roller skate a scooter. He cooks jelly from sour green apples and fashions a bow and arrow from bamboo. One afternoon, he's shooting emptied tin cans off the headstones, his brother dutifully gathering the fallen cans in a burlap sack, when his elbow slips. The arrow veers left, nicking his brother's right bicep, but it's no problem. There's nothing the subject can't solve with a little resourcefulness. Over Ebbie's muffled sobs, the subject tears his T-shirt into strips and applies a makeshift tourniquet.

*

A modest brick schoolhouse on Laurel Street. The subject reads Bacon and Virgil, argues with teachers, plays saxophone. When he questions creationism and the true authorship of Shakespeare's plays, his classmates are shocked; he doesn't care. Unlike his more popular and easygoing younger brother, he is determined to think for himself no matter the social punishments, a trait that does not endear him to faculty or students. He must question everything. He must imagine a better world and work toward achieving it just like President Wilson with his League of Nations. On graduation morning, he is adjusting his tassel in a hall mirror when the principal, a man of rigid social conventions like his parents, pulls him aside and surprises him with a warning: "You were born to be a leader of men. But never forget the value of human life." Later, he crosses the high school gymnasium stage and accepts a diploma from the same man. They shake hands firmly and lock eyes for a moment too long. The subject feels the principal drilling deep into him, turning over the parts of himself he can never see. How does the principal know him better than he knows himself?

*

A small liberal arts college in upstate New York. He takes walks by himself and writes poetry. But it is not so easy to buck social conventions here. He fears drawing attention in an environment where new fraternity recruits are tied to trees. After the other students ridicule his provincial accent, he tamps it down. *Do not do this, do not do that.* He tells himself he is not giving in to social control, merely excising a part of himself—the small-minded Susquehanna part—he has never identified with. Later, he will devise a term for this conformity through punishment: negative reinforcement.

*

A simple wooden coffin cradling the body of the subject's sixteen-year-old brother. The subject is nineteen years old, home from college on spring break. An ordinary April morning. They were eating drugstore sundaes in the parlor when his brother stood up and announced that he didn't feel well. Then back at home he fainted and the subject was calling a doctor and running for his parents at church while the ice cream was melting into the carpet and his parents were listening to the nice sermon, the chocolate syrup dribbling down his brother's lips while the blood was leaking in his brain, his perfect brother who followed all the rules and did not deserve punishment. When the doctor arrived, it was too late: the organism had expired. That was the only way he could think of this body that was no longer his brother. An organism. Expired like milk in his dorm room fridge. The organism had stopped being his brother the moment it expired because he did not believe in life after death, did not believe in the soul. *Never forget the value of a human life.* But there was no Ebbie left anymore, no life left to value, nothing beyond this corpse and the unconscious reflex behaviors of decay, and the subject was standing in the room's corner observing the four bodies assembled before him and their behaviors unordered by any mind. The organism's muscles relaxing into death, the eyelids losing tension, the pupils dilating, the skin paling and cooling. The doctor's hands removing the organism's shoe and touching the sole of its foot. The mother's arms embracing the expired organism and the mother's eyes blinking tears and the father's legs pacing and the father's lips muttering, "For heaven's sake. For heaven's sake," and the subject was still standing in the corner wondering why, if there was nothing beyond this body, why did the memories of the departed person surface when he stared at this lifeless form and why did he now remember shooting the organism with an arrow and the blood flowing just like the sundae's chocolate syrup, and why, if there was no soul and no Ebbie left, why why why did the organism's dilated eyes cause him to now remember feeding the organism's pigeons alcohol-soaked corn so they couldn't fly and would never reach heaven?

*

An artist's salon in his favorite professor's book-lined music room. The subject finds it's just what he needs after his disastrous first year of college. A little utopia far from his mother's mourning and his father's social striving, a heaven here on earth. In this house near the Oneida community, he listens to violin quartets and piano recitals, discusses astronomy and horticulture, falls in love with a banker's daughter. He mails his writing to Robert Frost and receives back an encouraging note. He dreams of a better life for himself, an artistic and intellectual life free from negatively reinforcing religion and social conventions.

*

A tiny but sunny writer's office at his parents' new home in Scranton's affluent Green Ridge neighborhood. Yes, his parents are moving up in the world even as the subject, at twenty-two and twenty-three, remains frozen in place, a recent college graduate trying desperately to become a writer. Over the next eighteen months, he goes through the motions. He builds a writing desk and a bookcase, buys a filing cabinet for manuscripts, and reads everything: Lewis, Proust, Wells, Pound, Madox Ford, Joyce, all the literary magazines. While his mother collects news clippings about kidnapped children, while his father's private law practice falls apart, the subject is caught between two more abstract desires: a prose like Dostoevsky's that expresses a philosophy of life through authorial editorializing and a prose like Chekhov's that is "pure" and "objective," that describes human behavior accurately and honestly, allowing the reader to interpret. Is it possible to have both? Although he admires Dostoevsky more, he believes he writes more like Chekhov. Since his brother's death, his writing has lost its more imaginative dimensions. Now the stones stay in place, and the mountain never moves. Now it's all description and external experience, the "reflex actions of reality," as he will later call them. He does not deny that emotional and mental states exist in the mind's black box, but he goes even beyond Chekhov's objectivity in his belief that writers cannot accurately portray their characters' thoughts and feelings. Writers cannot see the mountain moving stone by stone. Writers only guess, and the subject does not like this guesswork of imagining his character organisms' interior lives. Instead, he describes only their behaviors, never their thoughts or feelings. At night, he tosses and turns, wondering whether it's even possible. Can a literature that only describes physical behaviors ever express a philosophy of life? Is an honest description of reality even possible without reference to emotional and mental states? In the morning, he abandons page after page and builds model ships based on Coleridge's "Rime of the Ancient Mariner."

*

A windowless, temperature-controlled operating room. After watching his interest in writing wane, a family friend has invited the subject to consider a medical career. Dressed in white gown and cap, the subject watches the family friend slice into the patient. A tricky spinal surgery, the doctor had explained earlier. One false move with the forceps, and the organism prematurely expires. The statement's brutal simplicity doesn't concretize until the subject is sweating under the cold lights, watching man reduced to broken body, all chocolate syrup blood and chalky bone, the line between life and death, person and organism, so tenuous. When he stares too directly at the lights, he blinks. He does not think, *Blink*. The blinking's just a reflex, an uncontrolled bodily reaction like posthumous pupils dilating or hungry dogs salivating. Bright lights–blink, stimulus-response, stimulus-response. How is the mind involved with the body's behaviors? When have thinking or feeling or a higher spiritual plane ever demarcated lines between life and death? For months after the surgery, he cannot unsee the body from the operating room. He tries staring directly at the sun without blinking but fails. He reads Russell, Watson, and Pavlov. Here at last he finds an objective literature that still manages to express a philosophy of life, writers who understand that the world is only determined reflex and random accident, stimulus-response and one false forceps move. Better than Dostoevsky, better than Chekhov. He will become this kind of writer, he decides, one who accurately describes only physical reality and expresses a philosophy of science.

*

An open cockpit on a rainy flight from Switzerland to Belgium. He arrives drenched head to foot but smiling. It's not long after Lindbergh's solo transatlantic flight, and he's feeling daring. He has given up becoming a novelist, or at least this is the story he tells himself and others. He cannot know that he will write a novel one day. He has moved out of his parents' house in Scranton and will start graduate school in psychology in the fall. Now he travels around Europe without a care in the world. Now he doesn't just dream of flight. He flies.

*

A rented room across Harvard Yard. The subject maintains a rigid schedule: in bed at nine, up at six. As focused as ever, as regimented as his test subjects. Unlike his peers, he does not read the newspapers, does not observe Great Depression suffering or concern himself with elections. He breaks up with a well-read woman too similar to him. He breaks up with a poet. He electroshocks frogs to test their reflexes. He times rats running through mazes. He bikes to class and argues with his introspective psychology professors that there is no mind worth studying, no spontaneity, just animal intelligence and lawfully determined behavior. In the evenings, he sits at the desk he once built for fiction writing and records highly detailed descriptions of his test subjects' behaviors in a spiral notebook. In the filing cabinet he once kept for his in-progress manuscripts, he organizes folders of lab data.

*

A well-stocked campus workshop where the subject has everything he needs: a small milling machine, boxes of piano wire, circular saws and drill presses, machine screws in Salisbury cigarette tins. He spends hours here responding to this perfect environment and building devices for his experiments. A silent-release box operated by compressed air. A kymograph that records on clear gelatin. A mounted rat track that tilts like a seesaw.

*

A double-walled Celotex box with a one-way window. The subject bends wire into a lever that delivers food pellets from a glass tube and hooks coils to the kymograph drum.

He places a rat in the box. Arbitrarily, the rat pushes the lever and receives food pellets. The rat repeats the behavior and receives another reward. Then the rat pushes the lever faster and faster, forcing the kymograph's stylus to etch more acute peaks into the spinning drum. After collecting the results, the subject is elated: he has shown an organism can be instantaneously conditioned to lawful response with only voluntary behaviors and positive reinforcement. No negative reinforcement, no burning hell, no reliance on understanding the test subject's mental or physiological states. He has eclipsed even Pavlov in shaping new behavior rather than an existing reflex. This is the first operant conditioning chamber, the first Skinner box, the invention that makes possible the experiments that will make his career.

*

A hundred-foot kettle hole formed by melting glaciers. When the subject's lab environment overwhelms, when the introspective psychologists resent his success and reject his increasingly controversial ideas, he carries his dog-eared Thoreau to Walden Pond and contemplates a simpler life among the pine and oak woods and that heavenly blue ice that seems to go on forever. Seems to but does not. He knows it does not because Thoreau writes about measuring the pond's depth with a cod line and stone. Like a good scientist, Thoreau dispelled the bottomlessness myth with hard data. Thoreau's contemporaries were bothered by this, believing it destroyed the pond's loveliness, but the subject does not agree. He does not believe Thoreau's measurements make the pond less lovely just as he does not believe studying external behavior over cognition or physiology makes the organism less lovely. *What is love,* he will later write, *except another name for the use of positive reinforcement?* "On the contrary," he tells the beautiful organism he will one day marry, as they walk around the pond hand in hand, speaking of literature and gazing into each other's eyes. "On the contrary, certainty *is* lovely."

*

A 457-page volume detailing the subject's operant conditioning theory, *Behavior of Organisms.* When the book is widely criticized for ignoring physiology and past research, he doubles down on his ideas: cognitions are merely behaviors, all behaviors are environmentally determined, the mind is a black box. *Why do they not understand this?* he asks himself over and over. There's no time for doubt. He's just started a new teaching job in Minnesota, just married and become a father. One night, his wife gently brings up the criticisms. What if he's wrong? They've just gotten the baby to sleep and are about to ready for bed themselves, whispering so their daughter does not wake. He looks into her listless eyes, follows her stooped body's contours beneath the nightgown folds, the body that seems to shrink and pale each day. Yvonne does not enjoy life as a Midwestern faculty wife; she has reiterated her desire to return East, even suggesting he soften his position to obtain a better teaching offer. "But I know I'm right. I'm as certain as I am of my love for you," he whispers, believing she will find the sentiment romantic. But his words do not have their intended effect. She rushes to the bathroom. Muffled sobs trickle through the locked door, then the baby begins wailing. Two negative reinforcements on his behavior. *I will have to condition them to associate me with more positive stimuli*, he thinks, and resolves to change his behavior. Every day for the next week, he buys her fresh flowers and cooks dinner. Her eyes lighten. She stands up a little straighter. At week's end, he places a leather writing notebook on the dining room table and encourages her to pursue her dream of becoming a published writer. Slowly, she forgives him, and they settle into Minnesota life. They take turns reading Trollope to each other, return to taking long walks in the woods and watching the pigeons scatter as they approach. At the university, he builds a devoted graduate student following. He starts thinking again about how his ideas might apply outside the laboratory, how one might condition human behavior to build a better world. He starts reading the newspaper again.

*

A cramped passenger car on a Chicago-bound train. En route to an academic conference, the subject contemplates the recent Warsaw aerial bombings. The League of Nations, lacking both positive and negative reinforcement mechanisms, has failed to maintain peace. As he stares out the train's window, the Midwestern scenery rushes by like so many news images he would rather forget: the white smoke coating Warsaw like freshly fallen snow, the majestic churches and hospitals reduced to rubble, all those ashen-faced organisms prematurely expiring. So much negative reinforcement. It all makes him sick, so sick, or is he just experiencing motion sickness from staring out the window? He closes his eyes, breathes deeply, and only feels worse. Here he is, attending academic conferences and experimenting with rats while whole cities are destroyed! Can behavioral science principles not help improve the human lot? Can positive reinforcement not prevent the premature expiration of the human species? He opens his eyes and stares out the window again. A flock of pigeons is flying in formation, a V for *victory*, and they remind him of his brother's pigeons, the ones he prevented from flying. All these years later, and he still regrets piercing the organism with an arrow. Poor Ebbie, poor Ebbie's pigeons. If only he could prevent the Luftwaffe from flying too, bomb the bombers from higher up perhaps. But why not?

*

A strange idea for a pigeon-guided missile system. The subject knows the idea sounds absurd but pursues it anyway. Pigeons are *devices*, he tells himself. Devices with excellent vision and maneuverability, easily trained through reinforcement. His idea could save countless human lives if it works, maybe even end the war, and he's buoyant with optimism. After returning from Chicago, he buys pigeons from a poultry shop and gets to work. At the university lab, he slips the birds into sock and pipe cleaner straitjackets that restrain their wings and feet but allow head movement. With graduate student assistance, he teaches the birds to peck a target—an aerial photo of a Stalingrad intersection enlarged from *Life* magazine—and rewards them with corn. Later, after he receives grants and workspace from General Mills and the National Defense Research

Committee, he teaches the birds to peck touch-sensitive screens that will rest in the missile's nose cone and activate electrical contacts for steering. When the birds peck the center, the missile will fly straight. When the birds peck off center, the missile will change course. Eventually, he trains the birds to track moving targets, pecking four times per second, at simulated flight speeds. He simulates explosive battle sounds, turbulence, gravity, and altitude changes. He stuffs each mock missile with three bird pilots and appeals to the NDRC for more funding. Everyone tells him he's crazy, even Yvonne. She does not understand why he spends long hours on what she views as an outlandish, quixotic project, neglecting her and their young daughter. When she asks him to spend more time at home, tells him it's important that he do so, he's stunned. He tells her his pigeons will save lives, hundreds of thousands of lives, maybe millions of lives. What's more important than that?

*

A small black box with a viewing tube and round translucent window facing a slide-projected aerial image of New Jersey. Thirty-five hours ago, the subject harnessed the pigeon inside the box. Now he's making his funding pitch to skeptical NDRC organisms in a windowless Cambridge conference room deep inside an airless government building. Loosening his collar, the subject speaks confidently. After many months, he finally has the lingo, the engineer-talk needed for the NDRC organisms in dress uniforms. Pigeons are not organisms but machines. "We have used pigeons, not because the pigeon is an intelligent bird," he tells the committee, "but because it is a practical one and can be made into a *machine*, from all practical points of view." Blank stares, a few smirks. One NDRC organism with owlish glasses and a crew cut points at his wristwatch. He asks if they can begin the demonstration, says they're short on time. The subject smiles and asks the engineer organisms to gather around, but they're impatient. The same organism with the crew cut removes the black box's top to speed things along, flooding the target image with too much light. Even under these stressful new conditions, the subject is pleased to observe his pigeon pecking perfectly at the moving target. When the same organism with the crew cut purposely blocks the projector with his hand, the pigeon stops. The subject's heart nearly stops, too. When the organism removes his hand, the pigeon resumes pecking, and the subject exhales. A brilliant performance, absolutely flawless. The subject turns off the slide projector and stares around the room, expecting positive reinforcement. When he is instead met with further smirks, his heart sinks. The engineer organisms are not impressed. What's happening inside their black boxes? Can they not see the device works and will save lives? They cannot. Several weeks after returning home, he receives a letter denying further funding: *Further prosecution of this project would seriously delay others which in the minds of the Division have more immediate promise of combat application*, they write, alluding to weapons whose magnitude he cannot begin to imagine.

*

A makeshift laboratory tucked into the half-floor space at the top of an old General Mills flour factory in downtown Minneapolis. Time to clear out, pack up. Outside, screeching trains spew hideous black smoke that slips through the window opening, seeping into the subject's threadbare wool sweater and congealing at the back of his throat before finally crawling catlike into the pigeon cages and turning the birds restless and wild. On the roof, water tanks beam sunrays and a thirty-foot neon red sign looms in looping cursive—*Eventually*—because the slogan's "*Eventually* you will try Gold Medal Flour...so why not now?" *Eventually* the sign's six hundred and twenty-five light bulbs will burn out, and you'll undertake the treacherous climb to replace them amid freezing temperatures numbing your nail-bitten fingers, vicious winds tearing your unshaved cheeks, and snow so unrelentingly blinding you wonder if you'll ever see again. *Eventually* the pigeons will grow so distressed that you'll whisper softly to them, you'll lift them one by one from dropping-strewn cages, you'll nestle them to your chest and carry them to the open window and release them into the inky night sky. *Eventually* you'll have to accept that Project Pigeon is over, that your pigeons are gone, that you've not built heaven but sunk deeper and deeper into a shared hell, that you're not flying, that you're instead tied to the train tracks and the war's hurtling toward you, wailing and whistling and whipping down the tracks too fast to brake so there's nothing you can do to stop it, nothing but burrow deeper into the dirt, deeper into this earthly hell, holding your shallow breath and shuttering your teary eyes and praying with all your blackened heart—though you have not prayed in years—that it just misses you, that it just misses all the organisms tied to all the tracks in all the cities of the world and that you will live another day, that night will end and you will one day stand up from the tracks, staring into the bleeding sunrise and wondering what became of your beloved pigeons and *why not now?* Why was it not your time to die? Why are you still alive when so many have perished?

*

A fully enclosed, climate-controlled baby crib with three sound-absorbing metal walls and one safety-glass window. Now that Project Pigeon is over, the subject returns to real life. Yvonne is pregnant with their second daughter and overwhelmed by the care of their first. She asks him again if he can spend more time with his family, if they can return to how things were before. This time, he agrees. He tells her he wants to simplify childcare—to simplify matters for her and their daughter—and that he has an idea. In the basement, he rolls sheets over a canvas floor and winds them to a crank so soiled bedding can be easily changed. He filters moist air through the canvas floor and builds a temperature and humidity control box. He measures his wife's height so she will never stoop to lift their child. In this special crib, his daughter will stay warm in only a diaper and will move freely and safely. She will catch colds less often, will not suffer diaper rash or require as many baths. Her skin and posture will improve. Loud noises will not disturb her. Meanwhile, her mother can continue her day without worry or resentment. Certain such thoughtfulness will please his wife, the subject leads her down to the basement and shows her his invention. *Voilà*, the "air crib": a controlled infant environment allowing more freedom for mother and child! Beaming, he awaits positive reinforcement. She bites her lip and massages her swollen belly. He doesn't know how to interpret these behaviors.

Why is she not more pleased? After all these years that he has loved her, she remains a mystery.

*

A dinner party at the home of a prominent miller and socialite. The subject is talking to a family friend whose relatives are stationed in the South Pacific. He asks her what they'll do when they return, but the question pains him. He thinks about Project Pigeon, of course, and what will come next for him. The family friend doesn't know what her son and son-in-law will do when they return home. "Such a shame," the subject tells her. He thinks of Yvonne wincing every time she writes *housewife* under occupation on government forms, having long abandoned her literary dreams. "Such a shame if these young Americans return only to fall into the same conditioned patterns." Marriage, children, steady job, mortgage, the old lockstep like rats running through mazes. When the family friend asks what they should do instead, he blushes remembering his own failures. Then he tells her they should experiment and explore better ways of living. Like Thoreau, like American organisms have always done, like the perfectionist movements in Alice Taylor's book. She stops him mid-sentence. He should write his own book, she says. His own book about experimental communities to help the young people returning home. He laughs and shakes his head, but that night, after the babysitter leaves and Yvonne is asleep, he watches his daughter sleeping in the air crib. She is so safe here, so safe and healthy. He doesn't want her to learn of war. He doesn't want her growing up like her mother, dreams dashed on the pavement. Can he design a better world for them both? Can he save lives and end the war another way? For the first time in many months, he remembers his released pigeons and wonders what became of them. He places his hand on the warm glass, almost close enough to touch his infant daughter.

*

A planned community governed by positive reinforcement and behavioral engineering, simple living and self-sufficiency. Although the subject originally attempts an essay defending planned communities, he instead writes the fictional book that has long eluded him, only it's more polemic than novel. In a white heat lasting seven weeks, he rediscovers the imaginative dimension of his youthful writing without faking his characters' internal thoughts and feelings. Instead, he describes a perfect agrarian community free from religion, government, and capitalism. A community without private property, wages, or competition. A community where no one lacks food or sleep, both sexes share domestic labors equally, and the least desirable tasks are rewarded the most labor credits. In Walden Two, the community raises children, and adults only work four hours per day. In Walden Two, force and punishment are nonexistent. There's the *feeling* of free will if not the reality. The organisms all feel they are making choices even when they're merely conditioned to make those choices. They ignore the black box. When he closes his eyes, the subject can almost see Walden Two. As he writes, he can't help thinking this book is only the beginning, the blueprint for a better world. There's no problem human beings can't condition themselves to solve eventually, if only they forget what human beings are. No small feat, but they can do it. They can condition themselves like he has. Become fully equal organisms. End the war. The subject cannot possibly know that the war will end soon without his help. As he adds the book's final touches, he cannot know that another organism faces an impossible and unprecedented choice: Will he drop the bomb on Japan? Will he push the lever to receive his reward as he's been conditioned? Will he show the entire world that his country possesses the power to destroy not only this particular enemy in this particular war but to destroy humanity itself? To mutually assure the species' own destruction through the most human of impulses? No, the subject cannot possibly peer inside that organism's black box. For now, he is dreaming of flight, imagining an alternative future where bombs and missiles are obsolete, where there's no overpopulation or famine and no one's brother dies at sixteen, where the black box remains closed and positively conditioned human animals avert humanity's inexorable march toward catastrophe.

*

A utopia without war, hunger, poverty, or inequality. Finished writing, the subject asks Yvonne if she'll read it. He has written it for her after all, for their marriage and family. He tells her he'd especially value her opinion as a fellow writer, and she blushes, clearly flattered; she has not thought of herself as a writer in years. Over the next week, she works methodically, reading just a chapter at a time in the wicker chair by the unlit fireplace after dinner. Stone by stone. One evening, he's grading student assignments at the kitchen table when she enters the room. The subject cannot know it's the same evening Truman orders the bomb dropped on Hiroshima; the president will not make an announcement until the following day, after the city's already destroyed. He hears Yvonne's soft footsteps on the linoleum before he sees her, wire glasses perched on her nose and cropped hair falling into her eyes. She lays the manuscript on the table. A soft plop. The light flickering blue from the muted television in the corner. He sets his pen down and looks up, his heart beating loudly in his ears. Her expression is blank, her arms still at her sides. She hesitates before speaking, carefully choosing the words to break his heart. "It's hell," she finally says, pausing. When she speaks again, her words are quick and confident, water rushing from the dam after all these years. "I wouldn't live here. I wouldn't let our daughters grow up here. You've lost sight of everything human beings are, all the good in this world. I'm sorry, but you have to destroy it. It terrifies me." After she disappears into the back of the house, he sinks into the wooden kitchen chair, his whole body shocked, his arms hanging limply at his sides. After all his hard work, that's all she has to say? Can she not recognize the novel's brilliance? Does she not understand that a better world requires conditioning away from the human? Her words echo in his mind, an endless loop. *You've lost sight of everything human beings are.* For the first time in many years, he remembers his high school principal's warning. *Never forget the value of human life.* The memory surfaces. He's back at high school graduation, cap falling off his head and gown too long, standing in line to receive his diploma in the stiflingly hot auditorium. At last, they're calling his name, and he's climbing the stairs and crossing the stage to the principal. He's staring into his doughy face. He's shaking the sweaty palm with his right hand and accepting the rolled diploma with his left. The diploma's paper feels surprisingly lightweight, inexpensive. He's trying to smile. His parents are in the audience somewhere trying to take his picture, but he can't see them; the lights are too bright. *Blink.* The principal is whispering congratulations, but he can't hear it over the applause, can't even hear his own labored breath, and instead keeps hearing the man's stunning, earlier words. He returns to the kitchen table, the manuscript lying before him, and the fluttering, sour feeling in his gut. How closely Yvonne's words resemble the principal's! Coincidence, or have they both glimpsed an essential flaw? He scratches his head, wondering how they did it. How did they both manage to penetrate his mind so deeply when he can't do the same? Why can't he identify the flaw himself? He feels the way he felt then, like a rodent running through a maze in a glass cage, his every move carefully observed and recorded. He was not always like this, he wants to tell them. If only he could transport them to his past, make them inhale the dry heat of his grandmother's old stove or taste the ice cream dribbling from his dying brother's lips or recoil in agony as the surgeon slices into the patient. Perhaps then they'd understand that he was conditioned to be like this. His behavior was shaped, rewarded in successive approximations of a target. He is not wicked because he doesn't believe any person is wicked; they only behave wickedly. He is certain that, with practice and diligence, he can unlearn these behaviors, that he can reverse the conditioning until something inside him changes, too. Slowly but surely, stone by stone. The part buried long ago in the black box, waiting all these years to break free and fly away.

***

HOUSTON, WE'VE HAD A PROBLEM

We see Joseph Gordon-Levitt weaving through New York City traffic on a battered, white fixed-gear bicycle. Gordon-Levitt is playing WILEE the bike messenger, WILEE the disaffected Columbia Law graduate, WILEE the underdog protagonist who face-plants into a taxi windshield in PREMIUM RUSH. Or maybe we see Anne Hathaway riding around London in ONE DAY. Hathaway has just called EMMA's love interest and told him she's on her way and sorry about being so snappy this morning. We see Hathaway's back as she rides away from us. We see Hathaway getting smaller and smaller. Then we see Hathaway exit the blind alley, and we hear the screeching truck's tires an instant before we see it, we see it, we see it sweep her out of the frame. Or maybe we see a BICYCLIST pedaling hard uphill on a poorly lit country road in a sleepy college town, but no, that's too vague. He is not just a bicyclist, he is a PROFESSOR OF POPULAR FILMS. He is not just a professor of popular films, he is a MIDDLE-AGED, PHYSICALLY AVERAGE ADULT MAN. He is BRUCE. He is MY BRUCE. He is a bicyclist and a professor of popular films and a middle-aged, physically average adult man I dated five years ago, after both our marriages ended in divorce, but have not spoken to since and who

thus, USED TO BE MY BRUCE, though I will just call him BRUCE
now for simplicity. Regardless, we see an eighteen-wheeler
run BRUCE off the poorly-lit country road in the sleepy
college town. We see BRUCE somersault through the air
in slow-mo. We hear the tires screeching and the driver
cursing and BRUCE's bones crunch-colliding with the
pavement. We see a bird's-eye view of BRUCE sprawled
on the edge of the road. He is wearing faded Levi's rolled
at the cuff, his signature red bow tie, and a tweed sport coat.
No helmet.

This was no film. There were no stunt doubles, no cameras. Real blood trickled down BRUCE's pale, unsculpted
forearms. But when the hospital called ME after he was
stable, when the hospital called ME and asked if I could see
him, when the hospital called ME because his only living
relative was an ELDERLY AUNT holed up in a nursing home
halfway across the country, when the hospital called ME because, quite frankly, he must have forgotten to update his
emergency contacts after our breakup, when the hospital called ME because, to be even more frank, he was ap-
parently still not on speaking terms with his EX-WIFE and
had no one else, not a single relative or friend or halfway
dependable acquaintance except for ME—RACHEL, his es-
tranged EX, an ANXIOUS MIDDLE-AGED WOMAN HAVING A BAD
HAIR DAY—I couldn't help thinking it already sounded like
a movie. And not a very good one.

The morning of the hospital visit, I lingered
in the hallway and peered through the window to his room.
I didn't know what to expect. How do you talk to someone you haven't seen for five years, especially after a horrible accident like that? What if he wasn't the same person?

I was wearing a tan coat and black jeans and thought of MICHAEL visiting VITO in THE GODFATHER. BRUCE was sitting up in bed, a large bandage wrapped around his head, tubes snaking from his nose and arms to blinking machines and liquid-filled bags. Many university COLLEAGUES and STUDENTS had sent get well tokens. Cards, balloons, flowers. Everything untouched.

I stepped into the doorway. When he saw ME, he smiled and quoted CASABLANCA.

> BRUCE
> Of all the gin joints in all the towns
> in all the world, she walks into
> mine.

Same sense of humor, same spinning silver film reel eyes. Same old BRUCE, just more wrinkles and gray hairs.

"I've been worried about you," I said, pulling up a chair. "How are you feeling?"

> BRUCE
> (smiling) Shaken, not stirred. After
> all, tomorrow is another day! I'm the
> king of the world!

I bit my lip. GOLDFINGER, GONE WITH THE WIND, TITANIC. We had watched them at his apartment all those years ago, the humid summer air drifting through the open window, our hands clasped around sweating bottles of pale ale. Something was wrong, and my face must have betrayed my suspicions.

> BRUCE
> (*frowning*) Why so serious?

I leaned forward but couldn't meet his eyes. I stared at my feet. "Bruce, do you know what day it is?"

> BRUCE
> I told you. I wake up every day, right here, right in Punxsutawney, and it's always February second, and there's nothing I can do about it.

He was staring at ME the same way PHIL stares at RITA in the diner scene from GROUNDHOG DAY. Calm, resigned, a little sad.

Later, the DOCTORS confessed they were stumped. There was no brain damage, and all the scans and tests showed BRUCE's mental faculties were completely intact. The DOCTORS had no idea what was causing his condition, how to fix it, or how long it might last. They predicted BRUCE just needed time to recover. He would snap out of it eventually, but he would need help when he was released from the hospital. He had no car and had let his driver's license expire years ago. He was terrified to ride a bicycle again. SOMEONE would need to drive him to the SPEECH PATHOLOGIST. Given his inability to communicate with others, SOMEONE would need to help him at the grocery, the pharmacy, the convenience store. SOMEONE would need to be his TRANSLATOR. That SOMEONE would be ME.

That SOMEONE would be ME because he had no one else, and I had nothing else. Nearing early retirement from my nine to five at the Parks Department, I was biding my time with no future plans. My CHILDREN were grown, my FRIENDS were boring, and my CATS hated my guts. Since BRUCE and I broke up, I had dated a little but nothing serious.

Three days later, I picked him up from the hospital and drove him home. On the drive, I turned on the radio so we wouldn't have to speak. BRUCE stared out the window, drummed his fingers against his knee. When we pulled into the driveway, he stopped drumming his fingers and sighed.

BRUCE
There's no place like home.

He lived a few miles from the university, a ramshackle apartment on a quiet street just like I remembered. Same sad hedges, same stupid lawn gnomes. He had lost his house key on the bicycle ride, so I used the spare. Still hidden under the same doormat after all this time.

Inside, little had changed. Sun-stained film posters plastered the walls, and dust-coated monographs lined the bookshelves. He still had the landline phone and the stacked print newspapers and the VHS player. Chinese takeout cartons in the garbage, chipped coffee mugs in the sink. No pictures of his SON. No pictures of the EX-WIFE he had recently divorced when we started dating.

Seeing the dishes in the sink, he shrugged sheepishly.

> BRUCE
> *(winking)* I ate his liver with some
> fava beans and a nice Chianti.

I laughed. He was clearly embarrassed by the disastrous state of the apartment but trying to make light of it. This was one quality I had always loved about BRUCE: before his SON's accident, he'd had an amazing, self-deprecating sense of humor.

He reached for the first chipped coffee mug, but I lifted it from the other end. Our fingers grazed.

"Why don't you go rest?" I said. "You've been through a lot. I can clean up."

He seemed genuinely touched as he put the dish down.

> BRUCE
> *(grateful, squeezing my shoulder)*
> I have always depended on the kind-
> ness of strangers.

Over the next few weeks, we fell into a routine. On the way to work, I would drop him at the SPEECH PATHOLOGIST. GOOD MORNING, VIETNAM! he would say, slipping into the passenger seat, or I LOVE THE SMELL OF NAPALM IN THE MORNING. On my lunch break, I would pick him up again, and we would run errands. Determining our shopping list and route was always challenging since he could neither speak sensibly nor write nor read. HOUSTON, WE HAVE A PROBLEM, he would say, pointing to an empty milk carton or a squeezed-out toothpaste. Eventually, I pasted logos for the grocery, the pharmacy, and the convenience

JIM LOVELL
Houston, we have a problem.

Years ago, when I first saw the movie with BRUCE, he'd paused here. "My students are always surprised to learn that line's incorrect," he said, smiling. "The real astronaut said, 'Houston, we've *had* a problem.'"

At the time, I didn't know why he bothered telling ME this. Only now do I more fully appreciate the difference between a present problem and a present problem with a past. Now all these years later, BRUCE pressed pause again. This time, he didn't comment on the line. There was no need. He threw the remote on the floor, and then he leaned over and kissed ME.

As spring drifted into summer, we fell into old habits. We were HARRY&SALLY and ROSE&JACK and SCARLETT&RHETT and ILSA&RICK. We saw movies at the theater. Ate at nice restaurants outdoors. Strolled along the lake holding hands. He was not the best conversationalist, it was true, but I still enjoyed his company. It was just like those early years of our relationship, an uncomplicated love neither of us had expected after our divorces. Everything felt so right. Sometimes, I had to remind myself why we'd broken up in the first place: his SON. He had died in a terrible car accident after BRUCE and I had been dating a few years, and BRUCE was never the same afterward. He never talked about his SON's death with ME, not even once. He grew cold and distant, watched his films for hours and hours without stopping to eat. Forgot birthdays and anniversaries and DOCTOR's appointments. Talked about the CHARACTERS like they were real people, FRIENDS of his. I begged him to talk to ME, begged him to see a THERAPIST, but he only retreated deeper into his films. Eventually, he barely spoke to me at all. *He's mourning*, I told myself. *This will pass*, I told myself. But it didn't.

Eighteen months after the SON's accident, I reached a breaking point. There was nothing I could do to help BRUCE, and I couldn't live like this. BRUCE was in the living room, eyes glued to the screen, taking notes on PULP FICTION for the millionth time.

"Bruce," I said. "Bruce, I need to talk to you."

He didn't look up. I yanked the television cord from the outlet, and the image fizzled to black. "Bruce, I can't do this anymore."

He didn't say anything, just nodded like he'd known all along. He helped ME gather my things in a cardboard box and take them to my car. The toothbrush I kept in his bathroom, the paperback novels I'd lent him, the shirts I kept hanging in his closet. He didn't stop ME. He didn't defend his behavior. But just before I left, he grabbed my hand and held it to his chest. "Rachel," he said, speaking to me for the first time all day, "all this. It's not me."

His voice was hoarse and earnest, each word as deliberately chosen as the film posters lining his walls. Long after I stopped speaking to BRUCE, after other relationships came and went, a part of ME still thought of those final words and wondered what would have happened if I'd given him a second chance. Now I might have that opportunity.

As the school year approached, a pin burst our happy balloon. BRUCE was making little progress in his speech, and it was becoming harder to dodge calls from the university.

One Monday morning in July, we ran into BRUCE's COLLEAGUE at the convenience store. "Bruce," the COLLEAGUE called before we could escape. "Bruce, how are you feeling?"

BRUCE smiled, but I could tell he was nervous. He swallowed hard. Repeated the same lines from that day in the hospital.

> BRUCE
> Shaken, not stirred. After all, to-
> morrow is another day! I'm the king
> of the world!

The COLLEAGUE looked taken aback. She recovered and faked a smile. "Well, I'm certainly glad to hear that. We look forward to having you back."

The day only got worse. When I picked BRUCE up that afternoon, the SPEECH PATHOLOGIST sat us down in her office and said that BRUCE should stay home for two days. "I really think it will be best if everyone gets a little rest. Why don't we start back on Thursday?"

I looked at BRUCE, but he turned away. "What's the problem?" I asked the SPEECH PATHOLOGIST.

"Oh, have you not noticed?"

I shook my head. BRUCE avoided my eyes.

The SPEECH PATHOLOGIST explained that BRUCE's range of quotes had grown smaller over the last few weeks, that he was now only quoting IMDb's Top 100 Greatest Movies of All Time. "This is normal in a patient's recovery from a devastating injury like this," she explained, her voice sympathetic. "We like to think of recovery as a straight line, but often there are regressions."

On the ride home, BRUCE didn't say a word. When I asked if he wanted ME to stay over, he shook his head no. He was muttering the Houston line when he slammed the car door.

On Thursday, I returned to pick him up for his appointment. He was drunk, unshaven, and still in his bathrobe, empty beer cans strewn everywhere like a scene from ANIMAL HOUSE.

"Bruce, what are you doing? You've got a session today. You need to go. You need to get better."

He inhaled deeply, licked his lips, hiccuped. When he reached across the doorframe to clasp my hands, his eyes were soft and pleading, JACK TWIST in BROKEBACK MOUNTAIN.

BRUCE
Rachel, all this. It's not me.
Inside, I am... I am more.

I drew my hands back like I'd touched something hot, those familiar words taking me back all those years ago to our breakup. He was right of course. It wasn't him speaking. It was never him, I now realized, not when we broke up for the first time and not now. It was BRUCE WAYNE. It was BATMAN. It was Christian Bale and his perfectly chiseled jaw, loose strands of wet hair arcing across his forehead.

BRUCE, DEEP DOWN YOU MAY STILL BE THAT SAME GREAT KID YOU USED TO BE, I said, repeating RACHEL's lines from the film. BUT IT'S NOT WHO YOU ARE UNDERNEATH. IT'S WHAT YOU DO THAT DEFINES YOU.

His cheeks flushed red, and he slammed his fist against the door, shaking his head.

```
              BRUCE
Houston, we have a problem. Houston,
we have a problem houston we have
a problem we have a main bus B
undervolt-
```

I held him by the wrist. His hand trembled. He stared at ME with those spinning silver film reel eyes, and still he was the same old BRUCE, had always been the same old BRUCE. "Houston, we've *had* a problem," I corrected him.

∗∗∗

LOST IN THE DESERT OF THE REAL

Such would be the successive phases of the image:

it is the reflection of a profound reality;
it masks and denatures a profound reality;
it masks the absence of a profound reality;
it has no relation to any reality whatsoever;
it is its own pure simulacrum.

—Jean Baudrillard, *Simulacra and Simulation*

It's after the rush. After the New Year's tourists have packed their bags and the big golf championship has ended, but before the Martin Luther King Day vacationers arrive next week.

It's after fire and fury and Rocket Man. After North Korea has conducted its most powerful nuclear test to date and the American president has pledged total annihilation before the United Nations. After experts have estimated the missile could travel the nearly 5,000 miles of ocean to Hawaii in under twenty minutes and cause up to 18,000 deaths and 120,000 trauma and burn casualties. After the Twitter sparring, the town halls, the pamphlets and siren tests, the televised warnings to get inside and stay inside, the stockpiling of plastic sheets and gallon water jugs, air masks and two week supplies of canned goods. After experts have predicted the missiles would likely target population centers like Chicago, Los Angeles, and New York and that the fatalities in just one of those cities could reach six figures.

It's after all that. After the sun has risen on another lazy Saturday morning in paradise, another morning of January sunshine and gentle breeze. At Honolulu International, temperatures are in the low seventies but will rise another ten degrees by late afternoon.

*

Five thousand miles east of Hawaii, shielded behind a chain-link fence and a perimeter of seven hundred royal palms, past the thick hedges, valet-parked Ferraris and Cadillac Escalades, the quarter million dollar application fee, the marble foyers and crystal chandeliers, the private helicopter, the antique Venetian cherub statues, past hundreds of coconut trees and southern oaks, past the stone blue rivers and gently cascading waterfalls and white-sand bunkers scalloped into sloping fairways, watched by countless security cameras and tanned multi-millionaires in pastel golf shirts, surrounded by aides and Secret Service, artificially elevated by three million cubic yards of earth moved over nine months to create the highest course in the state, between the fourteenth and fifteenth holes of the exclusive Trump International Golf Course at West Palm Beach, the president blinks.

He has just seen something in the hedges. He *thinks* he has just seen something but isn't sure. His stomach growls. It is thirty-two minutes before the false missile alert in Hawaii, thirty-five minutes before the president's lunch, and one week from the one-year anniversary of his swearing in. A perfect 71.1 degrees with just a touch of humidity, leaves lifting in the west-northwesterly breeze, sunrays piercing scattered clouds.

The president blinks again and stares into the foliage. This time, he's sure he sees it: that mirrored eye he'd recognize anywhere, the dull gray-black plastic of the video camera, the worm of a man tangled in earbuds and microphones and wires. *Probably CNN*, he thinks. *Fake news. Fake news spewing more lies from Michael Wolff's recently published* Fire and Fury.

*

Five hundred miles away from the president's golf course is the town of Seaside, a master-planned community that became the set of the 1998 satirical science fiction film, *The Truman Show*. The film is not about the president who ordered the nuclear bomb dropped on Japan but about Truman Burbank (Jim Carrey), a thirty-year-old insurance salesman and "everyman" star of the most popular reality television show of all time, *The Truman Show*. Truman has spent his entire life on Seahaven Island, a fictional seaside town within a dome equipped with thousands of cameras that record his every action. Truman has no idea that his entire life has been filmed or that all the people he knows—even his mother, even his wife—are paid actors.

*

At the emergency operations center in Honolulu, the phone rings. Employee 1 leans back in his rolling office chair. He has just begun his shift. He sits at a tan metal desk facing four computer monitors: two with maps, one with security cam footage, and one for the controls. Pea-green Post-it notes litter the monitors. On his right, three plastic phones with red lights are blinking. A little metal fan clipped to the surface of the desk is pushing air around the small, cramped office. Employee 2 picks up the handset and transfers the call to speaker.

This is not a drill, says the voice.

Employee 1 will later claim he did not hear the first part of the message, that the crucial first words—*exercise, exercise, exercise*—were lost as the call was transferred to speaker.

This is not a drill, says the voice, and Employee 1 believes it. He believes it is really U.S. Pacific Command. Believes Hawaii is really under attack. He does not understand that the voice is only a recording, that it is not really U.S. Pacific Command but a midnight shift supervisor, Employee 4, running a drill. Twice before, Employee 1 has confused drills with real-world events. From a drop-down menu now, he selects the template for a live missile alert.

*

In two days, the governor's office will release an image of the alleged menu with a newly added false alarm option.

BMD False Alarm
Amber Alert (CAE) – Kaui County Only
Amber Alert (CAE) Statewide
1. TEST Message
PACOM (CDW) – STATE ONLY
Tsunami Warning (CEM) – STATE ONLY
DRILL – PACOM (CDW) – STATE ONLY
Landslide – Hana Road Closure
Amber Alert DEMO TEST
High Surf Warning North Shores

In three days, the Hawaii Emergency Management Agency (EMA) will dispute the first image and supply a second one. As these officials will point out, the second image is not the actual interface but a "close facsimile." It too has the new false alarm option.

1. State EOC
   1. TEST Message
   DRILL – PACOM (DEMO) – STATE ONLY
   False Alarm BMD (CEM) – STATE ONLY
   Monthly test (RMT) – STATE ONLY
   PACOM (CDW) – STATE ONLY

Later, EMA officials will falsely claim Employee 1 pushed the "wrong button."

However, as either image of the interface makes clear, there is no physical button that triggers a ballistic missile alarm just as, contrary to the president's Twitter boasts to Kim Jong Un, there is no "nuclear button."

If there were a nuclear button, it would resemble the pin button worn by Truman's lost love interest, Sylvia.

HOW'S IT
GOING
TO END?

From the drop-down menu, Employee 1 selects the template for a live alert. *Are you sure you want to send the alert?* the menu asks, and he selects *Yes*. He glances at the calendar hanging to his right—Photoshopped palm tree silhouettes leaning against an airbrushed sunset, fluorescent purple bleeding to aquatic orange at the horizon line—and then he checks the large overhead LED clock. Only a minute or two has passed since the phone rang.

$$08:07$$

Across the state now, thousands of smart phones light up with push alerts.

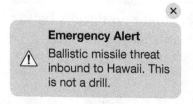

Emergency Alert

⚠ Ballistic missile threat inbound to Hawaii. This is not a drill.

A woman is sipping her morning coffee when she receives the alert. A commuter is driving southbound on the H-2 toward the H-1/H-2 merge. A University of Hawaii professor

is frying an egg for his three-year-old, and a mother is getting her daughter ready for an ice-skating lesson. A local
is paddling about twenty minutes offshore. At Hotel Wailea
in Maui, a guest is slicing a yellow passion fruit over a bowl
of yogurt.

*

Back on the golf course, the president retucks his white polo
shirt into his khakis and tugs the brim of his red baseball
cap, shielding his eyes from the sun. No one can make him
wear sunglasses. Not his fake doctor, not his chief of staff,
not even his daughter or son-in-law. He'll go blind before
he wears them, stab his own eyes out with his thumbs.
Sunglasses are for Crooked Hillary plotting Benghazi on her
Blackberry from a State Department plane. Sunglasses are
for Crooked Hillary slipping in and out of Chipotle
in Maumee, Ohio. Sunglasses are for the weak, for delicate
movie stars and seniors with glaucoma. They can't make
him wear them. He'll stare straight into the solar eclipse
if he wants, will scowl now at the fake news cameras and the
lying mainstream media until they scuttle away in shame.

The president blinks, the CNN cameras roll.

The one and only time he wore sunglasses was for the
June 10, 2016 issue of the *Hollywood Reporter*, a feature interview with the great traitor Michael Wolff just before
the California primary. Even those sunglasses were fake,
Photoshopped over his famous squint. Hope had loved
that cover: his disembodied head in gray scale, floating
over a grainy peach background slashed with red stripes
and a square blue patch decorated with dollar signs instead of stars. In the mirrored carrot-orange shades, his

rivals screamed into congealed crowds of sign-wielding immigrants, helmeted riot police, blackened palm trees, and suited men with video-camera faces, none able to match his calm, his serenity, his all-knowing California cool. The sunglasses should have tipped him off that the interview was nothing more than strategic flattery, the first drop in a bucket of lies, all part of Wolff's elaborate con and flawlessly executed betrayal, the apprentice upstaging his master in the season finale—if he weren't so mad, he'd be proud.

At the fifteenth hole, he places the ball on the tee, yanks the club from his caddy's hands, and swings. The small white ball vanishes in the sun's glare, and the Secret Service avert their eyes. The president's stomach growls.

*

On the mainland, a woman receives the alert at her office. She has just dropped her son at the airport and her husband at work. She has just picked up breakfast from the Nimitz Zippy's after looking at the menu for five minutes, agonizing over which Breakfast Bento to select.

Breakfast Bento (no substitutions)

#1: Corned beef hash, Spam, scrambled eggs on a bed of rice
#2: Portuguese sausage, Spam, scrambled eggs on a bed of rice
#3: Portuguese sausage, corned beef hash, scrambled eggs on a bed of rice
#4: Portuguese sausage, bacon, scrambled eggs on a bed of rice

Deluxe Breakfast Bento**: Corned beef hash, Portuguese sausage, Spam, scrambled eggs on a bed of rice. Sorry, no substitutions.

Now, she has an impossible decision: With whom should she spend her final moments, and will she reach them before the missile strikes?

Select a family member (no substitutions)

#1: Your husband, at his office
#2: Your two youngest children, at home
#3: Your eldest son, at the airport

In his private office, the Hawaiian governor paces back and forth. In his private office, the governor unbuttons his short-sleeve Hawaiian shirt because no one will see, and he is hot under the collar. In his private office, the governor is hot under the collar because he knows the ballistic missile alert is false. In his private office, the governor is hot under the collar because the alert is false and he knew this just two minutes after the alert and despite making all the right calls to EMA and others, he cannot remember his Twitter password to inform the great people of the great state of Hawaii on social media, where they will most certainly look first. He is the only one in the office at the moment. He has texted and left voicemails with his IT and Comms staffers, but no one has called him back yet. Sweat slides down the bridge of his nose, landing on the tongue of his right dress shoe. Warm, damp sweat patches sprout under his arms and blossom in the square of his lower back like yellow hibiscus, the state flower.

*

In Hawaii, there is no time to waste. Windows are latched, electronics unplugged, pets corralled. While her husband dresses their two children, a Kauai woman gathers cereal,

69

protein bars, cookies, apples, water bottles, toilet paper, and a cooler bag with turkey into a five-gallon bucket that will double as a toilet. On the lawn, the entire family shelters in a steel shipping container, and they stare at each other, and they don't know what to say.

Locals and tourists alike crowd into bathrooms and crouch in stairwells or under café tables. They scramble to garages and the rare basement or fallout shelter, break into buildings, huddle in hotel hallways, and fill the police stations. At the Foodland in Pupukea, strangers cluster around tomato soup cans. At Kualoa Ranch in Kaneohe, a newly arrived tourist bus is redirected from the legendary set of *Jurassic Park* to a far more terrifying concrete bunker in the mountains. Gathered for a reunion, five generations of a family cram into the laundry room of their rental home and soon begin to sweat from their collective warmth.

At the Longs Drugs near downtown Honolulu, a University of Hawaii professor and her husband squat on the floor in the toy section. Leaning against the dolls and action figures, they read books to their children and pretend that everything is OK, that they are in a real-life fairy tale with a happy ending. But the professor knows everything is not OK and has not been OK for quite some time because next week is the 125th anniversary of the American-led coup against Queen Liliuokalani. For years, the professor has argued that the overthrow of the Hawaiian Kingdom was illegal. For years, she has decried the American military bases that pollute the environment and make Hawaii a target for foreign adversaries. For years, she has spoken about how Hawaii's language and history and sacred lands are also under attack. For years, she has insisted that Hawaii is illegally occupied: governed by a false authority that denies legal reality.

*

In his private office, the governor paces back and forth and thinks of that other office, the ceremonial office down the hall where he signs documents to great fanfare, wielding the pen like a saber, slicing through the white space with a looping flourish. In the ceremonial office, he sits behind the curving half-moon koa desk and in front of the engraved state seal, the twinned American and Hawaiian flags, the pale, sand-colored curtains rippling behind him, beach waves cresting to bubbling white froth.

*

Five miles from the shore, a local is laughing with tourists on a snorkeling trip when the radio beeps, and the captain's face blanches. On a morning whale watching expedition off the coast of Maui, dozens of phones sound at once, and this captain is all smiles, eerily cheerful as he turns the catamaran around. When they reach the shore, everyone is calm. They will not see whales today. They dig their toes in the sand and await more information.

*

On *The Truman Show*, Jim Carrey's character and Sylvia dig their toes into the sand until Sylvia is dragged away from the beach, kicking and screaming that none of it's real. On *The Truman Show*, Jim Carrey's character digs his toes into the sand and remembers the sailboat accident that took his father's life. He is terrified of water.

*

Near Pearl Harbor, a cybersecurity expert starts running the faucets. He and his wife are filling the tubs with water. They are filling the drinking glasses and the wine glasses, the chipped coffee mugs and the dainty teacups and the plastic water bottles. They are plugging the sinks and filling them. They are lining garbage cans and dresser drawers with foil and filling those, too. They are filling the crusted metal pots, the glass mixing bowls, the glass carafes from the coffee maker and blender, the metal tins for pastries, the Brita filter, the measuring cups and mason jars, the mismatched plastic Tupperware, the emptied yogurt containers and milk cartons and cans of corn. They are filling Ziploc bags and garbage bags and plastic bags. They are adding more water to the dog's aluminum bowl and the fish's glass tank and the acrylic flower vases. They are filling mop buckets, suitcases, the washing machine and dryer, plastic rain boots, and canvas laundry hampers. They are filling their daughter's wooden costume box from which she stages elaborate games of make-believe and dress up, games with ruffled princess dresses and translucent fairy wings, glittering tiaras and sequined shoes.

*

In his ceremonial office, the governor buttons his short-sleeve Hawaiian shirt while a father in Maunawili dresses his daughter in a bulletproof vest. In his ceremonial office, the governor drapes an itchy lei around his neck while one of his constituents in Maui pulls his arms through an orange shirt so his body is easy to identify later. IT calls the governor back and tells him to contact Comms. A Comms junior staffer responds to his text, telling him to try his spokeswoman, Cindy. He calls Cindy, but she doesn't pick up. "How is it that *no one* has this thing?" he yells, slamming his phone down in disgust. He sits down at the koa desk, closes his eyes, and thinks about how he is the state's actor and the koa desk his stage. He imagines smiling for the cameras, an adoring audience slumped before him in pale, sand-colored armchairs. Under the white-hot lights and before the blinking cameras of this fantasy, he leaps across the stage and sings his crusted heart out. The bleached velvet curtains rustle and the jaded audience claps and he sings and he sings and he sings. He gestures at the orchestra pit and the audience claps and he gestures at the tech crew and the audience claps and then he finds his spot, he plants his feet, he bends at the waist, he slides his hands down the pleats of his dress pants, blood rushes to his head, and the audience claps and claps. Now he opens his eyes. He is still sitting at the koa desk. He still doesn't have the password.

*

Another performance: the president sitting down to lunch, unfolding the white napkin in his lap, wishing for his regular Big Mac and Filet-O-Fish. Since the Wolff book published those salacious details about his diet last week, his fake doctor and real doctor have been on his case, the first concerned more about appearances than health. Now he has to order the Mar-a-Lago turkey burger with sautéed apples, Tabasco sauce, and pear chutney or people will talk. Will say he's disgusting, unhealthy, so paranoid he won't even eat at his own club. He has asked the chefs to burn the hell out of the bird and to serve it with a side of ketchup, but it's not the same, no, it's not the real thing. Real doctor has also told him to exercise at least three times a week. *Exercise, exercise, exercise.* That's why he's here playing golf.

He takes a swig of Diet Coke, wipes his mouth on the back of his hand, sets the glass down. One of the military guys is approaching now. What's his name. They all look the same. Greased patty melt faces smothered in lumpy, fake-tanning-cream-colored special sauce, skin toasted and glazed with sweat butter, huge sesame seed pores leaking, beady gray pickle slice eyes blinking, a square of plastic gold cheese melting on the shoulders, diced green onions pinned to the collar, and wilted green lettuce ribbons fluttering just above the breast pocket. Military guy is saying stuff about Hawaii. Ballistics, drills, alarms, cheeseburger, cheeseburger, cheeseburger. The president does not hear the rest because his stomach is growling. He does not understand that a woman is sitting down to eat what she believes will be her last meal: a blackened pot of burnt rice garnished with sliced Spam rings.

*

Exercise, exercise, exercise. At the Ala Moana Center Planet Fitness in Honolulu, they are training to live forever while looking like they've never aged. For twenty-four hours a day, the treadmill tracks spin and the weight stacks clink and the exercise balls are thrown against the wall. For twenty-four hours a day, the Total Body Enhancement machine vibrates and glows with red light. For twenty-four hours a day, the HydroMassage water jets pulse and the tanning beds sizzle. For twenty-four hours a day, the customers climb infinite stairwells, bike miles and miles without moving an inch, and run on endlessly repeating tracks. Now everyone is running for their lives. Running in and out of the gym, running from the beach to the gym and from the gym to the locker room. Over in Mānoa, the university students are running from their dorms to Bilger Hall and its yellow fallout shelter signs. When they reach Bilger, they find the doors locked. There are no actual fall-out shelters on campus—the signs are left over from the cold war era—and so they run for the Marine Sciences Building instead.

*

Exercise, exercise, exercise. When Jim Carrey's character runs away from Seahaven, the producers do everything they can to stop him. First, they light fake forest fires, but Carrey's character races his car through the flames. Then they stage a fake leak at the fake nuclear power plant. Undeterred, Carrey abandons his car and runs through the woods on foot. He runs and he runs and he runs until the men in fake silver radiation suits finally capture him.

*

Exercise, exercise, exercise. In his private office, the governor paces back and forth. In his private office, the governor stares at the Twitter log-in page on his cell phone screen and types in password after password to no avail. In his private office, the governor curses the stupid blue Twitter bird. He imagines plucking out her feathers with just his teeth and feasting on her glistening meat, running his tongue over the delicate breast bones and crushing a blue

75

eyeball between his thumb and index finger. If only Cindy would call him back with the password. Cindy knows what he should say and how he should say it and how he should *look* when he's saying it and sometimes he wonders whether he's really the governor at all, whether the governor is not, in fact, Cindy, and sometimes he wonders whether, properly speaking, the private man behind the governor even exists and sometimes he also thinks about his mother giving him this body and this name, this life, and sometimes he wonders whether Cindy is not, in fact, also his mother because she has given him so much more than life: she has given him the *appearance* of life. And then he cannot help wondering—does the Twitter bird even have eyeballs, and if so, what does she see?

*

On Nimitz Highway, a U-Haul customer sees the door. He has just returned his rental and asked if he could shelter inside. After they kick him out, he lies in the parking lot and stares straight into the sun waiting for the missile to land and wondering if his two-year-old daughter and fiancée are safe.

*

On 'Ewa Beach, the state representative and his wife lower their four- and eight-year-old daughters into the bathtub and tell them to pray. The older daughter asks if they're at war, and the state representative tells her *Yes, yes we are, yes we have always been at war due to Hawaii's historical position as a military target.* When the mainland provokes foreign countries, Hawaii is the first line of defense.

The state representative has grown used to alternate realities: living in the present and past simultaneously, living as a man of the people and a man of God. Now the parents hold their daughters' hands and recite the Hail Mary. *Hail Mary, full of grace. Our Lord is with thee. Blessed art thou among women, and blessed is the fruit of thy womb, Jesus.* The state representative knows the words by heart, but when he gets to the part about Jesus, he cannot go on. His daughters are staring at him, wondering why he has stopped, and he wants to tell them about the war. He wants to tell them that Hawaii is like the Son, sacrificing again and again for the sins of the mainland. But is the sacrifice joyful this time? Is it a willing gift? He doesn't know what he believes anymore. *Holy Mary, Mother of God, pray for us sinners, now and at the hour of our death. Amen.*

*

Employee 1 believes Hawaii is really under attack.

*

At the end of the movie, Jim Carrey's character sails toward the horizon, and the production crew pummels his sailboat with wind and lightning. When the crew objects, fearing the boat will capsize, the director orders them to keep going. Christof, the show's creator, is willing to sacrifice his pseudo-son to save his filmic world. He is willing to drown a human being on live television so the show may go on.

*

At an undisclosed location in Hawaii, a man in a burnt orange polo shirt and black Nike baseball cap kneels over a storm drain. In the grainy YouTube video that goes viral on social media, he looks like he's praying: humbled and prostrate, aging knees muddied, callused palms cupped to the skies. The footage is overexposed, all light areas scrubbed of detail and bleached to depthless, heavenly white. The beaten sky, the fronts of the doomed houses, the man's creased cargo pants. The man is motioning a small girl to walk toward him and climb down the storm drain, but she doesn't want to. She tells him she doesn't want to go in. She won't meet his eyes. She's tugging on her shirt and her striped leggings. Another man rests his hand on her back and steers her toward the first man and the hole. Finally, she walks to him, and she sits down. She does not hold his hand. She does not hold his hand because holding his hand will make it real. She lowers her feet into the hole one by one. She is wearing dark sandals with blue socks, but they are not the same blue as the blue of the Twitter bird.

*

In his private office, the governor watches the blue Twitter bird land on his windowsill. He has never seen anything more beautiful in his life. She is dimensionless and eyeless, an electrified robin's egg blue, a chlorinated pool blue, wing curves sharp as saw blades. She leans in and taps the glass with her beak, twittering softly: that coyly seductive high-pitched whistling *yoohoo* he'd recognize anywhere. The Twitter bird drills through his skin, sawing the layers of tendons and muscles, peeling him back like an onion and cradling his slick, quivering heart in her beak. He has never felt so seen.

*

On Sandy Beach, a man calls his children to say goodbye. He hangs up and has a heart attack.

*

Back at the emergency operations center, Employee 1 is in shock. Employee 3 has to grab the computer mouse and send the cancel message. Later, Employee 1 will describe the sensation as a full body blow. Like wandering lost in the desert for days without water. His limbs are lead weights no longer connected to his body, and he has to remind himself to breathe without choking on his own tongue.

*

In his private office, the governor finally receives a text from Cindy. The password is the name of his childhood pet. How could he have forgotten? Seventeen minutes after the false alert, the governor types in his password, tweets that there is no missile threat, and collapses back into the plush carpet. He takes a deep, glorious breath of fresh air, holding it in his lungs for half a minute before exhaling. The carpet holds him, rocks him like a baby. Back and forth, back and forth. Then he remembers he needs the Facebook password, too.

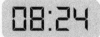

An agency meeting is held three minutes later to send out a correction. It takes another eighteen minutes to log on to the appropriate software and create a new template.

*

The president departs his golf course in a gleaming, armored limousine, disappointed that the false missile alert has forced him to cut short his golf game. In Hawaii, a high school math teacher receives a phone call from his daughter begging him to do the same. The teacher has just parred the last hole, he has just hit the crap out of his last ball, when his daughter calls to tell him about the missile alert, begging him to leave the fairway and seek shelter. He runs the numbers, decides there's no time. Instead, he flips the phone around and records a video of himself. He tells his daughter about hitting the crap out of his last ball, tells her he's going to keep playing golf if it's the last thing he does.

The teacher is not the only local who doesn't seek shelter. Some sleep through the alert or wonder why the sirens they have heard for months are suddenly quiet. Others are unfazed. An older couple, veterans of the duck and cover days, turn off their phones without reading the alert. In Honolulu, a lawyer assumes the alert is a joke and shrugs it off. In Mānoa, work continues as normal at the post office. A college student posts a screenshot for posterity and feeds his pets. A couple keeps walking their dog on Sandy Beach, a teenager continues with her breakfast, a husband keeps vacuuming. When his wife leaves to buy potting soil, they hug just in case. Some don't bother getting out of bed, others shrug and hop in the shower.

A Japanese-American Oʻahu native and army veteran closes his eyes and remembers Pearl Harbor. The slow-rumbling thunder, the white smoke chalking ink-black skies, all his ROTC theory and drills fading into the reality of battle: the reality of pulling the itchy uniform over his tanned arms and the reality of inserting the firing pins into the Springfield .03 rifle and the reality of grabbing the five-bullet ammo clip and waiting with his fellow Japanese-American cadets for the enemy paratroopers to descend over Mānoa Stream. Waiting for an enemy who looked like him. Quaking in the bushes and squinting in the sun, he could not have predicted the reports of paratroopers were false just as he could not have predicted the taunts, the internment camps, the assaults on his ancestry and patriotism. Over the years, he has grown used to the constant threat of attack. To living with multiple identities and in multiple realities.

*

On *The Truman Show*, Jim Carrey's character collages dozens of magazine photos of different women into a composite portrait of Sylvia. He can't seem to get the eyes right.

*

Thirty-eight minutes after the false alert, the second corrective alert finally goes out.

Emergency Alert

⚠ There is no missile threat or danger to the State of Hawaii. Repeat. False Alarm.

When it's over, they send the officers out with bullhorns. Missile drills are suspended, and an investigation is launched. In his ceremonial office, the governor apologizes and promises to get to the bottom of what went wrong. In Kealakekua, a veteran restocks her liquor cabinet. At the mall, strangers greet each other like old friends, swapping stories and abandoning their places in line. Over the highways, against a backdrop of sunlit palms and a foreground of mindless traffic, unreal signs with cryptic messages stretch toward the heavens.

> THERE
> IS
> NO THREAT

> MISSILE ALERT
> IN ERROR
> THERE IS NO THREAT

Four hours and one minute after the false alert, the president issues his first statement, tweeting from the @real account, "So much Fake News is being reported. They don't even try to get it right, or correct it when they are wrong. They promote the Fake Book of a mentally deranged author, who knowingly writes false information. The Mainstream Media is crazed that WE won the election!"

12:08

When it's over, Employee 1 appears on NBC, a shadowy silhouette with a slow, melodic drawl against a backdrop of glittering high-rise buildings distorted through the windows. The camera never reveals his face, but occasionally, the man is shown from the neck down. *Exercise, exercise, exercise.* He is wearing dark jeans and a short-sleeve button-down, faded plaid with a lighter floral overlay. His hands are clasped tightly across his lap. He is telling the reporter he thought it was the right decision, that he was convinced it was real. He does not know what he would do differently. For weeks, he has tiptoed through his life like a fugitive, a pretender, not quite here and not quite there, reminding himself repeatedly: This is real life. *This is not a drill.* Can't they see he feels terrible? Can't they see, can't they see, can't they see? As he talks, the buildings behind him seem to stretch and bend, sway and shrink. His right leg bounces involuntarily, and he clasps his hands together tighter and tighter. *Exercise, exercise, exercise.* He stares behind the young reporter at a framed painting of a hot-air balloon soaring past brilliant blue skies.

*

When it's over, Jim Carrey's character touches the brilliant blue sky. When it's over, Jim Carrey's character touches the domed walls of his prison, which are painted to look like brilliant blue sky.

*

When it's over, the president imagines himself in that hot-air balloon, soaring past brilliant blue skies, the wind licking his cheeks and the sun searing his back. In the master bedroom of the residence, an aide has connected laptops to the three flat-screen televisions so he can watch the 3D flyover simulations from his golf course website. Another aide has brought him the cheeseburger just the way he likes it: Quarter Pounder with cheese, extra ketchup, no pickles, fried apple pie on the side, silver tray.

His favorite 3D flyover simulation is from the Dubai golf course. Eighteen holes, five hundred acres in the middle of barren desert. They had said it couldn't be done, that he couldn't make the desert bloom. If he squints like the sun's in his eyes and stares at all three screens, the simulation almost feels real. Like he's soaring over the red sand and gently sloping fairways, like he's back in that desert where no one can touch him, that desert where it's not his fault, that desert where finally they're talking about Hawaii and not the Wolff book, and finally everyone sees what he meant about the fake news, and finally he can watch his three televisions and eat his damn cheeseburger in peace, and finally finally finally the president raises the burger to his lips. He closes his eyes and inhales the meaty ketchup smell, a warm tingling crawling from his nostrils down his neck and to his belly. Ah, nothing like the real thing. His desert oasis. Cheeseburger, cheeseburger, cheeseburger.

At long last, he bites into his enriched flour (wheat flour, malted barley flour, niacin, iron, thiamine mononitrate, riboflavin, folic acid), water, sugar, yeast, soybean oil, contains 2% or less: salt, wheat gluten, sesame seeds, potato flour, may contain one or more dough conditioners

(DATEM, ascorbic acid, mono and diglycerides, enzymes), calcium propionate (preservative), 100% pure USDA inspected beef, lettuce, soybean oil, pickle relish (diced pickles, high fructose corn syrup, sugar, vinegar, corn syrup, salt, calcium chloride, xanthan gum, potassium sorbate (preservative), spice extractives, polysorbate 80), distilled vinegar, water, egg yolks, onion powder, spices, salt, propylene glycol alginate, sodium benzoate (preservative), mustard bran, sugar, garlic powder, vegetable protein (hydrolyzed corn, soy, and wheat), caramel color, extractives of paprika, soy lecithin, turmeric (color), calcium disodium EDTA (protect flavor), milk, cream, water, sodium citrate, cheese cultures, salt, color added, sorbic acid (preservative), citric acid, lactic acid, acetic acid, enzymes, soy lecithin, cucumbers, water, distilled vinegar, salt, calcium chloride, alum, potassium sorbate (preservative), natural flavors, polysorbate 80, extractives of turmeric (color), and onions.

*

In three days, another false missile alert, this time in Japan. In twelve days, the Bulletin of the Atomic Scientists will adjust the Doomsday Clock to two minutes to midnight.

When it's over, the real Jim Carrey tweets, "I woke up this morning in Hawaii with ten minutes to live."

***

TONIGHT SHOW

George W. Bush is staring at the dust particles swirling in the bright studio lights. He is wearing a navy blue suit and red patterned tie. The mic is pinned to his left lapel, and he sits on a soft, tan chair with his hands clasped across his lap. Almost five years have passed since he left office. He is trying to look relaxed, at ease. Like he does this all the time. He *can't believe* he used to do this all the time. Jay Leno sits to his left, wearing a black suit and red tie, his white hair neatly coiffed, a tiny American flag pinned to his lapel. Across Leno's wooden desk, carefully positioned: another mic, some loose papers, a coffee mug. Behind them, through the windows: upscale office buildings, well-lit, purple tinted. They have just finished the easy topics. The joys of retirement. An update on Forty-One. Dubya's love of baseball. Throughout, the former president was as charming as ever, cracking joke after joke in his down-home drawl.

Leno leans forward, looks down. "Now, I know you've taken up some hobbies. You're *painting* now. You've shown me some of your paintings, and I was *very* impressed."

"I am a painter." Dubya nods.

"Oh, you *are* a painter now?"

The audience laughs, the camera zooms in. "I mean, *you* may not think I'm a painter. *I* think I'm a painter."

"No, but is it, is that second on your credits?" Leno jokes. "President of the United States," he raises his hand as if to place something on a high shelf, then lowers it, "painter?"

Dubya laughs quietly. "Well, it depends on whether you like the painting or not."

"No, they're very good. Did you take lessons or…?"

How did you start painting? Why did you start painting? Are you trying to communicate something deeper to us through the paintings? What do you feel? Since a hacker leaked photos of the paintings in February, no one has wanted to talk about anything else. He knows what the audience wants him to say. That he's guilt-ridden. That he's sorry. That the paintings are his way of reflecting on his presidency. Of soul-searching. But it's nothing like that. He never thinks about his time in office. Never thinks about the war or the made-up WMDs. Search for the meaning beneath the brushstrokes, he wants to tell them, and you'll come up short every time.

"I take a lesson from a woman named Gail Norfleet once a week in Dallas," he says, knowing this explains nothing.

He stares again at the dust swirling in the bright studio lights, the dust of West Texas, the dust of his childhood.

*

Ask anyone from West Texas, and they'll paint you this picture of the dust storms. Imagine it's late winter or early spring. The earth is dry, the soil loose, the birds long gone. With little warning, a wall of dust and debris sweeps into town. A big, black-brown, billowing cloud miles long and thousands of feet high. Your stomach sinks. Your ears fill with howling wind. You can't see your own hands. Miles above, pilots panic seeing the clouds. On the highway, drivers can't see the streetlights or over their hoods, and so the cars pile up. The dust seeps through every crack and hole, blankets every window. The crevices are plugged with wet rags until the houses ache with claustrophobia and static air and the weight of all those rags and still the dust seeps in. It stings your eyes and chokes at your throat, scratches you through your clothes. Every night, you place fresh sheets on the bed, but still they are brown by morning, still the pillow cuts against your cheek like sandpaper, still your life resembles more and more a sepia-toned photo, dim and hazy and prematurely aged.

Twenty miles from Odessa and forty from Big Spring, the small oil town where Dubya spent parts of his childhood suffers these dust storms. The summers are long and hot, the winters short and mild, but otherwise Midland looks the same year-round. There are few trees to lose their leaves, little greenery to redden in autumn. Fine dust layers coat everything. The checkered diner counters and creaking metal stools. The rusted big-haul trucks waiting in empty warehouse lots. The desolate oil fields where Dubya's father made his fortune. Ask anyone from Midland about the dust storms, and they'll flip through the yellowing, sweat-soaked pages of their pocket Bibles until they arrive at Genesis 3:19: *For dust you are, and to dust you will return.* Ask anyone from Midland, and they'll paint you this picture of a brown-tinged town stained with the aura of the unwanted and forgotten. A town sitting still for decades, waiting for some-one to pick it up, to shake off the accumulated years.

During the spring of 1954, Dubya's mother was growing dusty in Midland, too. Every morning, she sat in the living room gazing into the yard, the new baby asleep in the back room. Every afternoon, young Dubya found her in the same spot, dressed in the same uniform she'd worn since his sister's death that October: all black, her arms covered even though it was starting to warm again. She wore black shirts and black skirts. Black hats. Even black socks. She wrote with black pens in little black notebooks, slung a black purse over her shoulder, wiped her mouth with a black cloth, watched black birds flying past the window. Everything was black but her hair. Over the past few months, he'd watched her light-brown hair turn white—an unthinkable transformation in this dust-covered town, where new socks browned after barely a week. Sometimes, he wondered if her hair would change back. If his eyes were simply playing tricks again, like back in October when his parents picked him up from school in the middle of the day, when he thought he saw his sister's car seat in the back but was mistaken. His eyes were playing tricks on him then, too.

Today, it took Mother a moment to realize he was home from school. When she did, her face brightened. "Georgie," she called, using his pet name, "why don't you come over here and tell me about your day at school?"

Dutifully, he dropped his knapsack on the floor and crawled into her lap. He even let her kiss the back of his head though he was a big boy now, almost eight years old. He had still not adjusted to the new routine. For seven long months last spring and summer, Mother had been in and out of town. "In New York," Big George had told him afterward, when it was too late to matter, "trying to make your sister all better." Now Mother was home all the time. With Big George away so often on business, it was up to him to be the man of the house. To make her smile when he could.

"We had art today, and I made you this picture," he told her, unable to hide the excitement in his voice. From his pocket, he pulled a scrap of paper folded into quarters. Slowly, hands trembling, he undid the folds and began smoothing the paper. He wished it weren't so wrinkled. Yesterday, along with a letter from the grown-up relatives out East, they'd received a drawing from his cousin Hap. "To Aunt Barbara," an adult had written on the back in neat cursive. Hap's drawing was a landscape rendered via squiggle: green squiggles for grass, black squiggles for birds, a yellow squiggle for sunrays. Or was it lightning? He couldn't tell. It was a bad drawing, but at least the page was flat. Mother had smiled when she saw it, the first time all afternoon, and taped it to the fridge.

Dubya's drawing was much better than Hap's because it had people, which everyone knew were much more challenging to draw. It was the five of them—Big George, Mother, Robin, Jeb, himself—and they were holding hands. He'd tried hard making the drawing look as realistic as possible, even trading away his lunch so he could borrow a white crayon for the curlicues of Mother's hair and for the cloud, because he imagined heaven was like a cloud. The people had circle faces with dots for eyes and red U's for mouths. The smallest circle face person was on the cloud, and he'd drawn a skinny O over her head in gold, because angels needed halos, and Big George always called her his "little angel up in heaven."

He ran his hand over the page, trying one last time to smooth out the wrinkles before deciding the page would never lie flat. "Do you like it?" he finally asked.

Mother didn't say anything, just picked up the drawing and stared at it for a long time, tracing her right pointer finger across the circle faces one at a time. Her breath was warm against the back of his neck, and he felt his hairs prickle one by one. As he waited for her to answer, his eyes shifted to the mantle, where a painting of his sister hung. In the painting, she looked happy, just like he remembered her. She was wearing her pink Easter dress and sitting in a field of bluebonnets, her gold curls radiant against the dusty gray Midland landscape.

"Little George," Mother finally said, placing the wrinkled drawing back on the table. Her lips parted slightly, and he could see her tongue pressed against the back of her teeth, searching for the words. A soft, low-pitched wail echoed from the back of the house. "The baby," she muttered. The baby had been born just weeks before Robin became ill, and she never called him by his name. "Little George, why don't you go play outside for a bit? I have to get the baby." She nudged him off her lap, walked to her room, and closed the door with a soft click.

He stood at the door and listened as she shushed the baby. He knew she would stay in her room all afternoon and that he shouldn't take this personally. Mother had these moods and could not be blamed. Sometimes his tricks to cheer her up worked, sometimes they didn't. Thankfully Big George was returning home tonight from one of his business trips. Big George would know exactly how to cheer Mother up, and he'd also know how to appreciate Dubya's drawing. He imagined his father taping his drawing to the fridge, patting him on the back, and beaming with pride. Mother smiling. The three of them eating biscuits and chicken pot pie while the baby giggled in Mother's arms, one happy family again. If only imagining could make it real.

As he did most afternoons, Dubya left the house, gathered up some neighborhood kids, and found an empty lot. For the few hours they played stickball, he continued feeling hopeful. Only when he was walking back home did the feeling subside. He turned onto West Ohio Avenue. As soon as he saw the familiar gray siding and red roof of the family home, as soon as he saw the green Oldsmobile parked in the driveway and Big George's tall figure silhouetted in the front windows, he knew something was wrong. He could not say exactly what tipped him off, a slight change in the air pressure, the birds squawking overhead, the Oldsmobile parked ever so slightly left of center. He just had a gut feeling about it. As he got closer, he could see that the table was not set. That dinner wasn't ready. That Mother had not returned yet from the bedroom. He pressed his nose to the window and waited for Big George to notice him, but his father was too preoccupied, turning from the empty table to the empty stove, then back again to the table, where Mother had left Dubya's drawing.

Big George held up the drawing and stared at it for a long time, his face blank. This was not the man from the photo albums Dubya had pored over for hours, the smooth skinned fighter pilot and dashing young groom. His

father's suit was covered in a fine layer of dust, his briefcase battered, his shirt wrinkled, his hair greased back and
damp with sweat. He had loosened his tie, which now hung
unevenly off his neck. In the harsh lighting, his face looked
tired, bone thin. With his long, slender fingers, he folded
the drawing back into quarters, lined up the existing
creases, and slipped the drawing in the trash. Later that
night, while Dubya was tossing and turning in his twin-
size bed, after Mother was already asleep, he would hear
his father pushing a kitchen chair across the living room
floor. A soft scraping sound. In the morning, he would find
the painting of Robin lying face down in the dusty corner
of the room, a dark rectangle above the mantel where the
sun had failed to bleach the wall a lighter color.

*

"So here's the thing," Dubya says to Leno now. The studio audience is waiting. Dubya stares into his lap,
his voice as serious as it was on September eleventh.
"I want to share something with you. I *do* take painting
seriously, it's changed my life, and…" And is he really going to go through with this? He won't feign a remorse
he doesn't feel, one that would only open him to more at-
tacks, but he could offer them some small truths, reveal
something of himself. An understanding of loss. Shame for
his helplessness in the face of tragedy. The faint stirrings
of a long dormant interior life. But who would that help?
Why should he make himself vulnerable when it will only
make them feel worse, only make them remember all over
again? He feels a crinkling in the corners of his lips, the
old smirk returning, and he's back, he's Dubya again. The

Bombastic Bushkin. Joker and class clown. The candidate with whom the audience would most like to share a beer. The cowboy born of and returned to dust. It is so much easier to be like Leno, he thinks: to put on a show, to make them laugh so hard they forget they're bleeding.

"And I brought a painting for you."

"Oh, you did?"

From behind his chair, he retrieves an acrylic painting of Leno and holds it up for the audience to see. It's a view from the front. Leno's head is massive, easily filling two-thirds of the picture plane. The shoulders are cut off, the features flattened, the symmetry slightly skewed. Even so, it's undeniably Leno, right down to the coiffed hair, the purple backdrop, the little American flag pin.

The crowd goes wild as Leno reaches for it. "Oh, did you paint that? Oh, look at that." Leno holds the painting beside his doughy face and smiles for the cameras.

Dubya beams. He feels a warmth rising in his chest, the crowd's pulse surging through him like the best adrenaline, and he knows what they're thinking: *This is a good guy, a guy who can laugh at himself, a guy just like us. A guy we can forgive for tonight.*

***

FROM THE EYES OF TRAVELERS

I was at the AP Ankara bureau editing photos from a young Turkish soldier's funeral when my friend texted me the kind of photograph I would never take. Pastoral and sentimental, farmland with a heroic tractor and too-blue sky. Scrolling down, I realized it was a flyer for a photography exhibition. Later, the title of the exhibition would be translated in newspapers around the world as *Russia through Turks' Eyes* or, alternatively, *From Kaliningrad to Kamchatka, from the Eyes of Travelers.*

Exhibition, dinner after? read the accompanying text message.

I had not seen Ahmet in several months, our work schedules both being what they were, and the exhibition was on my way home. Still, I was tired. My eyes burned from hours of squinting at a bright screen in a dimly-lit room. I stared at the phone, unsure how to respond.

"*Kolay gelsin,*" said a familiar nasal voice from behind me. I turned and saw the metro desk editor, a pudgy, middle-aged guy with boyish features. For the last few weeks, he'd been filling in while the photo editor was on maternity leave and doing a terrible job. He apologized for forgetting my name again and asked me to remind him.

"It's Burhan," I told him for the third time that week, slipping my phone into my pocket. "Burhan Ozbilici. Oz for short."

"Oh, *Oz*, that's right," he said, scribbling on a notepad. "The wizard."

I nodded. Our enthusiasm for American films was one of the only things we had in common. During his first week supervising me, I'd explained that I was just like the man behind the curtain, always projecting frightful images through my little machines.

The editor smiled and peered over my shoulder. "OK, let's see what you got."

We scrolled through the funeral photos. The prime minister and opposition leaders, their heads bowed in prayer. The white-gloved soldiers bearing the red casket stamped with the star and crescent. After a dozen or so like this, we reached photos of the black-clad mourners. He asked me to slow down. As he leaned in closer to stare at the thumbnails, his breath fogged my screen, and I inhaled the small comforts of suburbia: stuffed eggplant, homemade yogurt.

"This one," he lay a finger on the monitor though I had already asked him several times not to do that—it smudges the screen.

I enlarged the photo so we could view it at full res. A portrait of a middle-aged woman, likely the dead soldier's mother, kneeling in the dirt, her head bowed in grief, forehead cupped in her palm. The photo was loose, ideal for a four-column placement. I had shot her high-angled and wide to emphasize her isolation and placement on the ground. Her mouth was open slightly, lip lines distorted in the harsh afternoon sun.

The editor covered his mouth and shook his head. "To lose a child. Devastating."

He had two children of his own, I now recalled, pimpled teenagers just a few years younger than the soldier. This was normal for desk editors, if not for journalists in the field. My three blue-eyed Siamese cats required little while I was away on assignment, only a daily check-in from a neighbor.

"Oz," he said, turning to me. "I just don't understand how you do it. Don't get me wrong. I admire the hell out of your work, but doesn't it get to you sometimes, taking these photos day after day?"

I shrugged. From the darkened computer monitor, my reflection stared back. The sun-stained wrinkled skin. The receding hairline and graying curls. Sometimes I stared at faded black-and-white film photos from my childhood and didn't recognize the knobby-kneed boy, his crazed hair and his ragged notebook, or the long-dead father whispering just over his shoulder. "Wild wolf," he would grunt, in his low smoker's rumble. "*Vahşi kurt.* Don't let the real wolves catch you." *Do not feel so deeply that you lose your way*, he was telling me. *Do not allow your outrage and lofty ideals to lead you astray.* When I see those old pictures now, I have trouble believing them. I can't remember myself as an idealistic youth, this wild wolf. Always I see the old man gazing through the young man's eyes. In my case, the wild wolf was never in danger of becoming the real wolf; he was in danger of losing his wildness altogether, of numbing himself to the world's evils.

"Is it really any different from what your metro reporters do at a greater distance?" I finally said.

"That's the thing though, isn't it? The distance. I don't understand how you get this close to a grieving mother and stay so detached." He touched the monitor again. I winced. "How do you get that close, take her photo, go home and sleep, wake up again, and do it the next day? Doesn't it affect you at all?"

I sighed. "Photojournalists either burn out or find ways to compartmentalize. We know when to engage and when to back off. I think of it as a professional oath of sorts, a personal code of separation."

He raised an eyebrow.

"Look," I pointed to two small, framed photos on the corner of my desk, one upright and the other flipped over, face down. "You see this one?" I tapped the flipped over frame. "It's from a Pakistani earthquake. To take it, I had to detach just like you say. That's the first part of my code. A good photojournalist must show what happened. Get the story, not interfere."

The editor reached for the frame, but I gently batted his hand away. "Trust me, you don't want to see it. It'll keep you awake. You've gotta be in the proper mindset."

He withdrew his hand, nodding solemnly. "I've never been very good at that. Compartmentalizing."

"Yeah, and that's also the problem. I've seen guys get so committed to observing, so numbed, that they forget how to feel. That's why I've got the other one." I pointed at the second photo, a Polaroid of a little Pakistani boy. "Injured in the same earthquake. I stopped shooting to help him, and his parents sent me this photo later, as a thank-you."

"Cute kid."

"Right?"

I stared into the kid's eyes, so bright and hopeful, and felt a tightness in my throat. "He reminds me to feel. To be human. No matter what I see. No matter how much I've gotta detach in the moment. Our empathy muscles? Just like any others. Use 'em or lose 'em. So I try to exercise mine a little each day. See from the eyes of those I photograph."

This was the key thing. This was why it would become so hard for me to talk about the photos of Mevlüt later. A good photojournalist knows when to abandon the curtain and when to remain behind it. When to feel as a man and when to remain detached and useful as a photojournalist.

I glanced up at the editor, hoping for understanding, but instead found his face etched with pity and confusion.

"That sounds really difficult," he said, his voice soft and pained. "I mean, I get it in the abstract, but to actually apply it. That's an awfully hard way to live, you know?"

I was not accustomed to such concern from a colleague. It was unprofessional, patronizing. I willed myself to disengage, cracking a smile so he wouldn't sense my discomfort. "Well, we've all got burdens, no?"

He straightened his posture, relaxed his expression. "Sure, I suppose that's true," he said. He tapped again on the screen, told me they'd run the photo of the grieving mother, and said he'd see me tomorrow.

After he left, I sat for several minutes silently seething, gripping the edge of my desk so hard my knuckles whitened. I knew I shouldn't let his earlier words bother me.

After all, he was a bumbling fool and had been a desk editor too long to understand. Still, his fatherly tone, his condescension—they stung. While he sat in his cushy, air-conditioned office editing stories, I was out in the field every day, risking my life. I had slept in the glass rubble and bathed in the bloodred rivers of earthquake-ravaged villages. I had knelt beside corpses, saliva bubbling on their chapped lips, eyes like silver fish scales. Who was he to judge me? To pity me?

The dead soldier, I was sure, would have understood. He had risked his life every day. Had known what it was like to live in two spheres, to shift from battlefield to home front. I scrolled back through the photos from his funeral until I found the one I wanted. The military processional. At the front of the line, a single white-gloved soldier carried a framed portrait of the deceased. I zoomed in until the dead soldier's face filled my screen. The portrait was official, military, cropped just below the shoulders. Smooth cheeks, clear eyes.

Yes, I was sure he would have understood me. Now it was my turn to understand *him*. To perform my exercise and see through his eyes, the editor's words be damned. Silently, I mouthed his name to myself. I recalled that he had been heading home for a weekend of leave when the car bomb detonated, killing him instantly. Twelve others had also died. A week earlier, anti-Erdoğan Kurdish militants had claimed responsibility for a similar car bomb in Beşiktaş.

I tried to imagine how badly he must have anticipated the upcoming weekend of leave. A weekend without the itchy flame-resistant uniform or the heavy waterproof boots, a weekend without shaving, a weekend without saluting, a weekend without marching, a weekend of his mother's red pepper stew and his warm childhood bed, a weekend of neighbors doffing their hats and thanking him for his service, and a weekend of long-lashed and long-limbed girls—the same girls he had long admired in school, the same girls who had long ignored him—listening with admiration, listening to *him*, as he spoke of the four a.m. wake-ups and the hundred pound backpacks, the drills and the marching and the way they taught you to crouch on the ground, to fire with one eye closed, to always look over your shoulder.

When I closed my eyes, I could almost see him riding the military bus with the other off-duty soldiers. He had the sweat-stained vinyl seat tilted back, his baggy-sweatpantsed legs draped across the aisle. Ray-Bans on to block the brilliant Kayseri sun streaming through the dust-streaked, December-frosted window. Wine-red Galatasaray baseball cap twisted backward across his smooth, buzzed scalp. He was smiling. He was talking to his best friend in the unit, passing him a pair of headphones, telling him he had to listen to this song, and then...

My cell buzzed with an incoming text. I opened my eyes. I was back in the Ankara AP bureau, tucked away in the soothing monochrome of nubby gray carpet and off-white cubicles, the gentle clatter of typing and the rustle of printed pages. Behind me, a fax machine beeped and whirred to life. A landline rang, and the occupant of the adjacent cubicle slowed her typing to answer it.

I glanced at the new text message from Ahmet.

C u there?

The prospect of returning straight home to my sad little apartment and spending the evening with only my cats now seemed particularly grim. I was no longer feeling tired but fired up, restless. It would be nice to see a friend and attend an art exhibition. Take my mind off work and the conversation with the editor.

I texted Ahmet that I'd see him there shortly and made a few final exposure adjustments to the photo of the grieving mother. Finished, I stuffed my laptop and lenses in my bag, checked for light meters and backup batteries, and slung a camera with a flash and fresh memory card over my shoulder. Technically, I was off the clock, but I liked having gear just in case. Given how many stories we'd run recently about Turkish-Russian relations, I might shoot a nice feature of some government officials the editors could peg to a news story later. Another part of the code: Like a good soldier, a good journalist must always be prepared.

*

When I arrived at the sleek Contemporary Arts Center in Ankara, I realized I was underdressed. The men wore crisp, dark suits and sported stylish facial hair that perfectly framed their square jaws; the women clutched tiny metallic handbags and glided like figure skaters in impossibly high leather boots. Everyone nibbled on goat cheese, crackers, and nuts and sipped from plastic cups of white Angora wine. Occasionally, they rested a plate or napkin beside a vase of poinsettias on one of the glass cocktail tables. Mevlüt was already there too, but I didn't see him just yet. As I was scanning the crowd for Ahmet, a warm hand squeezed my shoulder.

"Glad you could make it."

Ahmet and I embraced, lightly tapping our cheeks. Even though I saw him every few months, I was always startled by his appearance. We were the same age and had grown up just blocks from each other with similar dreams: he, to be a foreign correspondent, me, to be a photojournalist. Since then we'd gone our separate ways. He took a corporate communications job, married, had kids, sent them to university, divorced. Now he dressed like a man half his age and dragged me to poetry readings and art exhibits. Today, he wore a fashionable black sweater and blue contact lenses, his ear pierced with a single silver stud. His hair, thinning the last time I saw him, was now completely shaved off.

I pointed at the earring. "That's new, isn't it?"

"I've had it a couple weeks." He leaned in closer and lowered his voice. "Hurt more than I would've thought for such a small hole, but don't tell anyone I said that. The kids couldn't get over it, said now they'd have to take theirs out."

I smiled. "Here, let me take a portrait of you. This new look," I gestured dramatically. "At the very least, you can use it for the new dating profile."

As on numerous other occasions, Ahmet made a big show of protesting, then agreed to let me photograph him. I fired a few frames using a low f-stop to blur the background and flash to wash out his wrinkles. Then I flipped the camera to show him the LED screen.

"*Aman tanrım!* Is that what I really look like?" He clasped a hand to his mouth in mock horror.

"Best I can do. You're not so young, my friend." I pretended to greet him like a senior citizen, kissing his right hand and touching my forehead to it.

He was rolling his eyes and fretting over his appearance when another man approached. Like Ahmet, he was middle-aged but youthfully dressed with a gray bowler hat, matching vest, and impeccably trimmed goatee.

"Are you press?" he asked me.

For a moment, I was confused. Then I noticed he was staring at my Canon EOS 5D Mark III.

"Oh," I shielded the camera instinctively before loosening my grip. "I *am* a member of the press but not right now."

"Sorry, I have to ask." His voice was deep and theatrical. I wondered how he got the scar under his left eye—it seemed so perfectly placed, like stage makeup that transforms the handsome actor into a villain. "I work for the gallery, and we have special rules for photography."

"Special rules. Such as?"

"No bad pictures."

Ahmet and the man in the hat both burst out laughing, and again I was confused. Ahmet clapped me on the shoulder. "Oh lighten up, lighten up. He's just pulling your leg. This *fool*—I regret to call him a friend—doesn't work for the gallery. Far from it. He's actually just another corporate shill like me."

I smiled and turned to the friend. "Well, your act's very convincing. I can be a bit literal-minded sometimes, a casualty of the trade."

They both laughed, and the friend told me his name. Berat. I told him mine, and we shook hands.

"So you're an artist," Berat said.

"A photojournalist," I corrected him. "The artist should have a point of view. I just try to show what happened."

Berat grinned. "But isn't that also a point of view?"

These are the people I can't stand: the anything-goes relativists, the ones who throw the search for truth out so easily. I opened my mouth to respond, but he brushed me off. "Man, I'm just messing with you. A photojournalist, a photographer, whatever you are. I'm curious. What do you think of this exhibit, as a professional?"

I laughed, assuming he was joking—no one ever wants to know what the photographer thinks—but Berat didn't laugh with me. Then I realized he might be serious. Ahmet raised an eyebrow.

"You really want to know *my* opinion?" I asked, peering behind them both at the black-framed photos and the thin wire suspending them from the ceiling.

"Every now and then, the man isn't joking," said Ahmet.

"Really," added Berat. "I do."

We walked closer to the photos, only a few feet away from where Mevlüt, as I would later realize, was standing. Mostly, the photos were as bad as I'd feared. Idyllic Russian landscapes with traditional architectural elements. Gleaming onion domes and white spires spread across oversaturated blue skies. Green-rusted cannons carved with sentimental floral details. Technically sound but with no sense of drama, the same photos found in any tourist guidebook about Russia.

While I was struggling for words, a photo in the corner caught my eye. I moved over for a closer look. It was an image of a run-down little alley building under boarded windows, mostly copper or patina green. The dust-red bricks in the wall had faded to gray. Some had fallen out and been patched over with cement, like rotted teeth filled with cheap zinc-mercury. In the top right corner, a woman crawled through one of the windows. She wore metallic red pumps and a sleek, black skirt, her legs taut and her face hidden. The photographer stood maybe ten feet away, the camera roughly eye level, and I could tell the photo wasn't staged. Something was off about the angles of the wall and the color balance.

"I really like this one," I finally said. "It tells a story."

"That's one of my favorites too," said Berat. "I keep wondering if she's running *to* something or running *away* from something?"

"Or *someone*," I added. "She could be running away from the photographer. Happens more often than you'd think."

"That's interesting," said Berat, leaning in for a closer look. "Is this the type of photography you do?"

Ahmet answered before I could respond. "Oz only photographs suffering, ugliness, death..."

They both laughed, but I just shrugged. "It's the truth."

"So you must have plenty of work then," said Berat.

We all fell silent, and it was obvious all three of us were thinking of our troubled southern neighbor. I thought of the images from the halted evacuation of Aleppo, the ones that must have so troubled Mevlüt. The acid-green government buses and red-striped ambulance vans snaking through ruined buildings. The families sprawled at the feet of bearded men in military fatigues, grasping for food bags stamped with the Russian and Syrian flags. All those ashen-faced little boys with bandaged heads squinting through shattered windshields.

I lifted a champagne cup from a nearby table and drank deeply.

Finally, Berat leaned toward me, his voice lowered to a whisper. "Tell me, Oz. As a journalist, what do you think of this meeting of the defense ministers in Moscow tomorrow? Do you think we can really trust the Russians to uphold their end, or are the renewed talks just more of the same bullshit?"

"I don't see how it can work," Ahmet interjected, also keeping his voice low. "They have their interests, we have ours, and we're on the same side only when it's convenient."

They both turned to me. My pulse quickened, and my palms began sweating. Normally, I avoid political discussions because I don't want viewers to doubt the objectivity of my work. Still, this doesn't mean I don't have political opinions.

"Ahmet's probably right about it mostly being temporary," I said. "It's hard to trust Russia, but we have plenty of mutual concerns, too. Gas lines, trade, tourism, and besides, we really don't have a choice. We have to work with the Russians even if it's impossible to trust them. We have to stay involved in the region, defend our independence and keep the republic from breaking apart. So yes, I believe a measured diplomatic response is the best option."

Berat snorted. "As far as I'm concerned, the partnership will never work. I'm not sure I even believe in diplomacy with Russia anymore."

I paused mid-sip, and the words tumbled out half question, half statement. "You don't believe in *diplomacy?*"

He shook his head, the blood rising in his cheeks. "A bunch of old guys sitting behind closed doors smoking pipes while our young men are dying in the streets? It's only a matter of time before another Russian plane invades our airspace, kills our men, and then the conflict spills over into Kilis and Suruç again, all for the sake of Syria. It's bullshit. We can't have an ally who sides with Assad and violates our borders. You have to pick sides. You say your diplomacy is a measured response. Well, my friend, forgive me for being so blunt, but there's nothing measured about supporting Assad, is there? I mean, surely there's nothing measured about supporting a genocide?"

"No, of course not," I said. But I was taken aback by his accusations. It had been years since I'd heard someone speak like that, especially someone his age. The jaded photographer who feels too little and the wild wolves like Berat and Mevlüt who feel too much are equally frightening to me. Both have a tendency to slip into nihilism. How did he not see the difference between diplomacy and supporting the dictatorship? It was a dumb thing to say, a dangerous thing to say. I decided to press him, thinking he would shy away when he was forced to follow his logic to its disturbing end. "But I'm curious. You say you don't support diplomacy with Russia. What would you propose instead?"

"Oh, Oz, you don't want to know," said Ahmet. "Berat here fancies himself a radical now, thirty years after his university days."

"No, I *do* want to know," I said, a little louder than intended, though I was not angry, just confused. What other way was there? There was only force, diplomacy, or anarchy. From across the room, a woman in a blue blazer stared at us. My face grew hot. Berat's words had deflated me.

Berat dropped his voice to a whisper again. "You really want to know? I think we should get together with the Americans and sort things out ourselves. Bomb if necessary. Take out Assad. Hell, I don't even care if the jihadists seize control or if some civilians are sacrificed for the cause or if we completely destroy our relationship with Russia and start World War III. Why talk to the Russians when you can shoot at them?"

Berat winked, and I hoped he was again just pulling my leg. Certainly he couldn't believe something that insane. Letting jihadists seize control? Killing civilians? World War III? No one was that extreme, that off base. Before I could confirm my suspicions by asking him, a loud noise interrupted us. I turned and saw a man behind a podium tapping at a microphone. "Welcome, welcome, and thank you for joining us tonight."

"Ah, just in time," whispered Berat, nodding in the direction of the speaker. "We'll talk politics later. To be continued!" He smiled and patted me on the back a little too roughly.

"On behalf of the Contemporary Arts Center," the speaker continued, "I want to welcome you to this important photography exhibition, so relevant for our contemporary moment."

I turned my attention to the speaker. He was facing a video camera I had not noticed until then, and later, when the footage became widely available online, I'd pause with my finger on the play button, unable to bring myself to watch it. A few others stood behind him. A woman in a dark suit taking notes. An older gentleman who looked important.

I swung the camera body from my shoulder to my torso and raised it to my face. Once my hands slid into position, they stopped sweating. I loved the cool aluminum searing my skin and icing my hands, the way the figure came into focus as I rotated the lens. Compared to my normal assignments, this was easy. The gallery was well-lit, the white walls an automatic color corrector. I snapped a photo of the speaker, then a photo of the audience. A man to my left stared at the camera for a moment before deciding I was professional enough, that I belonged here. Even Ahmet nodded approvingly. With each click, my pulse slowed, my breathing steadied. I drove Berat's crazy words from my mind.

The first speaker finished his remarks and glanced just behind him, at the older gentleman who looked so important. "And now, it is my great pleasure to introduce tonight's special guest, the ambassador from Russia, Mr. Andrei Karlov." He ceded the podium, and the ambassador took his place, a translator by his side.

Before Karlov began speaking, I captured him with a fast shutter and shallow depth of field. He was impeccably dressed, regal as a lion. A navy cardigan and slate-gray suit jacket hid his round belly, and a spotted tie tamed the soft folds of his voluminous neck. Faint pinstripes raced from his shoulders to his feet, creating the illusion of greater height. He was a few years older than me but no more, with a wide, flat nose and thick, purplish-pink lips. His shining gray hair whitened at the temples, and a few sunspots freckled his olive complexion. Like me, he wore eyeglasses. Wire-rim aviator-style frames.

I made a few adjustments to the ISO and snapped another photo. Then Karlov began speaking. His voice was calm and quiet. Hands clasped behind his back, he enunciated every syllable, pausing occasionally for a translator to relay his words in Turkish. Even though I couldn't hear very well, he captivated me. His straight posture, his measured tone. After Berat's shocking words, after all the recent violence, it was comforting to see a man like Karlov. *This is a man who loves his country,* I thought, *an earnest man who commands respect but with the utmost humility. A rational, seasoned man who listens to all sides and doesn't let his passions sway his decision-making. Like a good photojournalist, he has a code that tells him when to feel and when to remain detached.* I imagined he had been a diplomat for many years, and indeed he had. How could whatever extremist character Berat was playing look at a man like this—at a man like me—and say he supported genocide? It was much more complicated than that.

Berat was not impressed. "Leave it to these self-important Russians to bring their own bodyguards," he muttered.

Berat tilted his head to the left. I followed his gaze, and that's when I saw Mevlüt pacing just behind the ambassador, hands folded across his chest. It's hard for me to separate what I now know about him from how I saw him then. In that moment, he just seemed so impossibly young. A monochromatic man-child with black suit and black shoes and black socks and black belt and black hair and black eyes and black brows and black heart. White shirt. White skin. White knuckles. White-hot rage.

Later, I would look at the photos and tell myself the facts. He's a monster, a murderer. And then I would force myself to do the difficult thing, the thing that would make me sick this time, the exercise that is necessary to uphold my code but that is so much easier with someone like the young Turkish soldier or Karlov, someone good and worthy of empathy: I would try to really see him while still holding him accountable for his actions. I would see the small Aegean coast where he grew up, a conservative cotton town caught between two eras. The oversize satellite dishes and remote-controlled AC perched over water-stained stone houses without indoor plumbing. The sand-colored strip malls beckoning with drooping palm trees and flickering fast-food signs: Burger King, Sbarro, Starbucks. The white cotton fields stretching for miles in all directions, the blue haze mountains lifting from the sea. The horse-drawn carriages meandering across dusty roads and the bronze travelers lazing in glossy resort pools, sampling skewered beef and cubed lamb, smoky grilled onions and slow-roasted tomatoes.

I would see the towering Levi's, Nike, and Adidas factories where his parents used to work, crouching over sewing machines until their backs ached and their fingers bled. I imagine they returned home smelling of formaldehyde, blue dye on their hands and bags under their eyes. I imagine they taught him to take good care of his clothes. To appreciate the difference between soft, heavy cotton and cheap polyester blends. I imagine he hung his uniform every night while he attended the police academy in Izmir, rolling off the lint each morning. That he ran his fingers across all his shirts checking for loose threads, little flecks of dirt. That he fell asleep watching those haunting images from Syria on the television, his seemingly innocent outrage over civilian deaths slowly congealing into a hatred of all that is human, a call to violence, permission to murder. How many more like him were there?

As the ambassador continued, I stared at Mevlüt. He was wearing a slim-cut suit, and his short, dark hair was closely cropped. His brows were dark and thick, and the rest of his pale face tapered from a wide, flat forehead. Smooth cheeks, clear eyes. As I would also later learn, he had flashed his badge and skirted the metal detectors at the gallery entrance, and so the metal was probably cold and heavy in his waistband as he paced behind the ambassador. I was used to seeing wild wolves like Mevlüt blend into the background. Usually they were bored, stared at their feet, fidgeted endlessly, but Mevlüt was calm and focused. He stared intently at the ambassador, drinking in every word. Only later would I realize what that look was. "Wild wolf," my father used to say. "*Vahşi kurt.* Don't let the real wolves catch you." Mevlüt was no longer just wild but a real wolf. His was a corrupted idealism that could only end in blood, the yellow brick road forking into the haunted forest, the dream turned nightmare.

Eventually, Mevlüt stopped pacing. He checked for something in his front pockets and crossed his hands over his chest. Then he raised his hand. He pointed the gun at the ambassador, and the gesture was almost cinematic. I heard a loud gunshot. The ambassador fell to the ground, just meters away from where I stood. The gunman calmly lifted his left hand and pointed to the ceiling. "*Allahu Akbar,*" he shouted in Arabic. Then, in Turkish, "Do not forget Aleppo, do not forget Syria!"

It took me a moment to register what had just happened: a man had just died, he had been shot in the back, there was no blood that I could see. My fingers trembled on the camera's cool metal.

Here's the thing. I've always known that the curtain doesn't exist. That my code is a lie. That one can never truly see through the eyes of another. A photographer in the assassin's line of fire isn't really objective. One cannot feel for the victim and remain detached enough to photograph his assassin at the same time. A photojournalist cannot remain both good and useful simultaneously. Berat was right that objectivity is a point of view, diplomacy a position. Looking back, I see I had two real options. Take my photos and abandon my humanity or take my humanity and abandon my camera. Take out the dictator and allow the jihadists to seize power or take out the jihadists and allow the dictatorship to continue. Terrorism or genocide, genocide or terrorism. But what kind of choices are those? What kind of world only allows for such choices?

I have refused many times and still refuse to accept such a world. Instead, I chose a third option: I pretended the curtain still existed. That I could be both good and useful, that a diplomat's words could still achieve peace in a world ruled by arbitrary assassin bullets and photographed by numbed cynics. I am Oz, after all. A hypocrite and a fraud. A believer in miracles.

I lifted my camera to take Mevlüt's picture.

That was when I heard the shouting, just like in the movies. And the other gunshots. At least eight gunshots echoing off the pristine white walls. All around me, people were screaming and running for cover, diving behind walls and under tables. The gunman was shouting and waving his gun and tearing photos from the walls. Had there been a little wounded Pakistani boy to help, I like to think I would have snapped out of my detachment and abandoned my camera. As it was, there was nothing I could do to stop the assassin, nothing I could do to help the other innocents in the gallery or the dead man himself. I could only take their photos, show the world what happened. In that moment, I summoned my best efforts at detachment. I did not allow myself to run. I did not allow myself to scream. I didn't think about Aleppo or the dead ambassador or Ahmet or even myself. In that moment, I pretended my crumbling curtain still existed, even as the first drops of blood were spattering my shoes, even as the wolves were devouring curtains left and right.

I had a job to do. I'd feel again later.

*

The rest of the night was a blur. Security eventually evacuated us outside, where ambulances and armored vehicles were already arriving. Later, I would learn the gunman was killed in a shoot-out with police. I quickly scanned the crowd for Ahmet and Berat to see that they were OK—we were separated during the evacuation—but I didn't have time to wade through to speak with them. I had to finish the job I'd started. On my way to the office, I called my editor to tell him what had happened.

"Can you get a picture?" he asked.

"No, no, you're not understanding. I was *there*. I'm headed back right now to upload and transmit."

He asked if I was OK, and I told him I was fine. Then I called the London editor and told her the same thing.

Back at the office, I had no time to edit my images because word had arrived from the higher-ups. They wanted me to write a firsthand account of what I'd witnessed ASAP. I transmitted the photos without looking at them, and then I typed up a statement and sent it to the bureau chief. When I was done, I finally allowed myself to breathe and drink a glass of water. My phone showed ten missed calls, all from Ahmet. I called him back, and he immediately lit into me. Where was I? Why wasn't I answering my phone? How could I just abandon him there? He could have been shot, he could have *died*.

I answered with a lie—a lie I wished with all my heart was true—and then a truth. "Ahmet, brother, of course I was thinking of you, I was thinking of you *the whole time* I was photographing. I wouldn't have rushed off unless it was really important, and it was. The world needs to witness what happened to you so it doesn't happen to anyone else." This answer seemed to satisfy him. We made plans to meet up later in the week, and I made plans to imagine later what he must have gone through, to empathize with his fear knowing it was no substitute for standing beside him.

After hanging up, I turned back to my desktop and really looked at the assassination photographs for the first time. How had I taken these? They were film stills, so staged and self-consciously artful. Scrolling through the first photos of Karlov speaking at the mic, I was shocked to see Mevlüt standing just behind him like a friend or bodyguard. I had photographed these shots as portraits of Karlov with a shallow depth of field. The shooter was out of focus but still fully present, haunting the left corner of the frame with a look of grim determination. It was the second-best photo I'd ever taken. I do not say this to flatter myself, only to acknowledge what's true. Even if I'd known what would happen in advance, I could not have photographed it better. I clicked through the remaining images. The bloodied martyr sprawled under the holy white lights, his body a perfect cross. The assassin brandishing his weapon and pointing to the heavens, vertically oriented and sharply focused. Why were they all so perfect?

I turned away from the screen, sick to my stomach. My hand drifted to the flipped over photo from the Pakistani earthquake, the one too horrible to describe. For the first time in many years, I turned it over. My hands were shaking and my heart felt like it would slide from my chest, but I forced myself to look. It was just like I remembered and just like I had tried to forget, the best photo I'd ever taken: haunting but beautiful, devastating but brilliantly composed. This is the key thing. Much as I try to pretend otherwise, there's a flaw in all my photos. They do not just tell a story. They show a point of view. They have always shown a point of view.

By now, the metro desk editor was by my side looking at the photos, too. "I feel awful for saying this, but the images. They're just beautiful, Oz. They really are."

"No," I said softly, pretending like I hadn't just thought the same thing. "You shouldn't say that. They *aren't*. They depict something horrible."

"I just don't understand how you did it, Oz. A man dies right in front of you, and you're composed enough to make these brilliant pictures..." His voice trailed off, and he covered his mouth, slowly shaking his head.

Behind his comments lurked the real question, the one that terrifies me, the one I hear in my father's voice, then in Ahmet's: *What happened to you, my wild wolf? How did you lose your wildness?*

Because it was the right thing to do, I wanted to say, because it wouldn't have helped anyone for me *to feel* in that moment, because to do the best thing at the time is still to be complicit in the larger wrong. Instead, I straightened the two photos on my desk, the flipped-over one from the earthquake that is too horrible to describe and the Polaroid of the little Pakistani boy. The little Pakistani boy who I only noticed and was able to help because—and thank goodness for this miracle—my camera battery had already died. "Like I said earlier," I told the editor, "I follow a strict code of separation."

***

THE AUTHOR AND THE HEIRESS

A screaming comes across the sky. It has happened before, but there is nothing to compare it to now.

But that's not true, thinks the Heiress, because you can totally like, compare it to her scream in *House of Wax*, a Teen Choice Award winner thankyouverymuch. The Heiress is the one screaming as she falls from the helicopter. She does not know the notoriously reclusive Author can hear her, nor does the notoriously reclusive Author know the scream is hers. The notoriously reclusive Author hears the scream in the distance. At first, the scream is high-pitched but faint, just a coal-black teakettle whistling. Then the scream grows into a full-throated, bloodcurdling, crystal-shattering shriek. A slasher movie screech, slimy dangling tonsils exposed, clammy neck hairs raised, chewed nails dug into sunburned scalps and trapped in the frequencies. A scream to make Edvard Munch proud, a scream to shame Drew Barrymore's Casey Becker, a scream of the markets crashing and the angels falling and the Rocket dismantling, the film running backward, the whole glittering hot-pink universe like like like collapsing back to its steaming, sparkly stiletto core. Now the water is at full boil, and if you don't hurry, it will spill over the coal-black teakettle's sides and set off the fire alarm, which is, like, pretty lame.

The Heiress is still screaming, clutching her tiara tightly so the wind can't lift it. No one will steal her crown tonight.

As the Heiress careens through the night sky, tonsils ablaze, the Author lies on his back, between the zero of sleep and the one of waking, eyes open and hands clasped across his chest, the bedside clock pacing the beats of his aging, mechanical heart. *Tick tock tick tock.* The ache of the Author's marble joints, the weight of his stone limbs, the pounding in his metal skull. Now the Author hears a loud crash on his fire escape. Now he hears profane bone on sacred steel, inanimate human colliding with animate machine at the speed of light, and the scream is gone. The Author blinks. The Heiress momentarily loses consciousness. It is 12:01 a.m. The Heiress rises and thinks, *That's hot, now it's my thirty-seventh birthday, bitchessss!*

*

At 12:02 a.m., Thomas Pynchon felt his wife tapping his shoulder. Could he be a dear and deal with whatever that noise was out there, because she had that important meeting tomorrow. The new Nicole Krauss book, did he not remember? Obviously he remembered. Obviously he'd be a dear. Obviously he knew Mel was suffering from a *One Hundred Years of Solitude*-esque insomnia plague and hadn't slept in three weeks, but, but—

"B-but what if it's…Them?"

That was it. He'd done it now. Eye mask off, earplugs out. "Tom, darling, how many times must I say it? A TV crew's not *really* trying to find you. Your characters aren't *really* trying to find you. That show won't make it to pilot. No one cares about postmodern novelists these days anyway, especially ones who haven't published new material in years. You know that, right?" He tried saying something in his defense, but she cut him off. "No, enough with the conspiracy theories tonight. Can you just handle it, whatever it is? It's not the people from that show." She squeezed his hand, and the electric current flowed from his gnarled fingertips up his arthritic wrists. "Please? For me?"

The pale-red alarm clock light flooded Mel's sallow, sleep-deprived skin, and he felt a stab of guilt. Lately, he'd put her through so much. Mel had not married this paranoid, delusional recluse, he reminded himself, but a man who merely avoided the press. In the early years of their marriage, he had still attended German expressionist film screenings with her at the neighborhood art cinema, holding her hand in the dark and waiting for the lights to turn on, to bathe them in dust halos. Back then, he had still gone with her afterward to the Italian restaurant around the corner, discussing the film over penne alla Norma and chicken parm, a tart Montepulciano easing his words, then walked home with her in the shallow moonlight, sharing a pistachio cannoli from a paper bag and whistling show tunes.

"OK, fine," he sighed. "But first tell me, why d-did the bee get married?"

Mel rolled her eyes, smiling in spite of herself, and they delivered the familiar punch line together: "Because he found his honey."

Tom climbed out of bed and grabbed his revolver from the nightstand. Punning aside, he was still terrified.

Breathing heavily, he padded into the den. Across the room, darkness shrouded the screen door to the fire escape, and the distantly rumbling garbage trucks and keening police sirens only added to his paranoid calculations:

$$(scream + sirens) \times dead\ of\ night = them?$$

"What d-did the ghost say when he wanted dessert?" he whispered to himself, tiptoeing over the hardwood. He and Mel lived in a tastefully decorated, highly coveted, prewar classic six on the Upper West, the Yupper West as he liked to call it. Oak floors, real wood-burning fireplace, and even a little writing office in the former maid's quarters. He hated himself for this sometimes, his hypocrisy after years railing against the Man and the System, wandering between motels in his stoner Greyhound days. If his old pal Richard Fariña were still alive, he'd consider Tom a sellout.

At the screen door, Tom lifted the gun from his waistband and placed his other hand on the doorknob. A cold shiver, an electric jolt, blood pounding his ears. He thought of his neighbors across the street, the weathered souls and wearied bureaucrats he hadn't seen in so long, holed up in their own apartments, everyone trapped behind bulletproof windows or corroding concrete, faces bathed in the blue television light, asleep or adrift or dreaming of an end, an illusion of an end, a salvation. Poor imprisoned and commodified souls. How he loved and missed them all!

Clenching the knob until his knuckles whitened, he counted to three. "I scream!" he shouted, flinging the door open.

*

Paris Hilton opened her eyes and gazed into the starless Manhattan sky. She didn't remember much. It was her birthday, yes. There was the helicopter, yes. Selfies in the helicopter to upstage Kim's Insta before arriving at the club. Then a loud bang, and where was she now? Lying spread-eagled on a fire escape? If Kim could see her now, Paris would die. Just *die*.

Pulling herself to her elbows, she peered over the guard-rail. She was several stories up a brick building, trapped on a rusted metal fire escape with stairs leading nowhere good. Below, rats scurried past a man wrapped in stained newspapers, a mangy oversize mutt pawed at a plastic garbage can, and a yellow cab squeezed through a stoplight. Cheap fast food odors wafted through the air. Light rain pattered gently on the metal platform beneath her feet, every solitary beat taunting her, reacquainting her with loneliness.

She shivered. This wasn't the birthday comeback she'd envisioned. For weeks, she'd planned the perfect entrance: a dramatic helicopter landing on the roof of Kim Kardashian's new club, the wind spilling her former assistant's drink down her expensive dress, the good old-fashioned frenemy fight rekindling the flames of Paris's fast-fading fame. After that, she was sure to land a new book deal, new reality show, new lover, new best friend, new *something*. Now her brand revival was all ruined. She'd have to get to the club tonight and cause a scene some other way before her birthday good luck ran out with the sunrise. It wasn't easy clawing your way back into the hearts and minds of the millions who'd forgotten you as quickly as last year's runway fashions. But on your birthday, you could do anything. Wear a glitzy chain-mail mini, have twenty birthday cakes, throw a party spanning five time zones. Anything was possible.

Come on, Paris. You can do this. Slowly, gripping the guardrail for support, she pulled herself to her feet and brushed the debris from her dress. Her clutch purse had vanished, but she was otherwise miraculously uninjured from the fall. She lifted her iPhone from her boob pocket and, noticing a new voicemail from Nicky, pressed play.

Hey, sis, it's me. I just wanted to wish you happy birthday. Hope it's the best. Sorry I couldn't come out tonight. You know how it is with a toddler. You should stop by soon though! I know you've been busy with business, but we really miss you. Call me? Here's Lily singing her Aunt Paris a happy birthday...

As her niece began singing, a warmth rose in Paris's chest. How adorable was Lily singing to her? This was the best birthday present, other than regaining the spotlight and having the whole world sing her happy birthday, of course. "No matter what happens in your life, never forget that you're a star," her beloved late grandmother had once told her, and when was Gram ever wrong?

Exiting the voicemail message, she extended her arm and admired her outfit reflected in the black screen. Diamond tiara, sparkling silver pumps, a sheer pink mini. Rule number eleven from her *Confessions of an Heiress* book: *If you're happy, wear pink.* Helicopter crash or no, failed reality show or no, she still looked *hot,* and this was the most important thing: to be desirable and glamorous no matter what, this millennium's Marilyn Monroe. WWMD, she always asked herself.

Lifting her chin, she pursed her lips into a pout, then relaxed into a smile. That was when she saw it, the large black gap where her front right tooth had been knocked out. Hideous! Like a creepy, unlovable witch. Strange that she hadn't felt it fall out—it hadn't even hurt. She clapped a hand to her mouth in horror. "My goodneth!" she lisped in her high-pitched mock-baby coo. "Thath *not* hot."

A door she hadn't noticed opened behind her, and a man yanked her inside the brick building. Was he kidnapping her, hoping for a ransom? She held her breath, heart pounding in her ears, legs trembling. But no, he was elderly and frail. She took a long, slow breath like the therapy chick had taught her to do during an episode. So he lived here? He had the absolute worst teeth she'd ever seen. Not that she was a kettle to call the pot black or whatever the saying was, but they were horrible. Bugs Bunny teeth, protruding and crooked. So *not* hot.

"Um, hello? That wath like, really rude," she lisped, rubbing her arm but winking, dusting him with her special Paris glitter so he wouldn't feel badly.

"Sorry, you c-can never be sure you're not being followed," the old guy stuttered in a thick Long Island accent.

"Thath like the whole point. Being followed."

The old guy grimaced, and she giggled a little. How could she have ever mistaken this snaggletoothed geezer for a kidnapper? He was not at all like those strange men from the boarding school who had woken her in the night as a teenager, slapping the icy handcuffs on her without explanation while her traitorous parents sobbed in the hallway.

"Why were you on my fire escape?" he asked, his voice weary. "And who the hell are you?"

Who are you? The question launched cold shivers down her spine. She knew he was asking in the literal sense—which was bad enough—but the night's strangeness lent his question a sharper, more sinister edge. She'd release thousands of new products around the globe, would spend every waking moment promoting her brand and producing new content, never resting, never having a moment alone, just to avoid this deeper question, the one asked in countless interviews: *Who are you* really? *What's the real Paris like like like when she's not playing Paris for the cameras? When she's not so focused on making us love her?*

She swallowed hard. "You don't know who I am? I'm on TV all the time. *Wath* on TV all the time."

The man shook his head. He told her he'd recently tossed his TV and didn't get out much—hardly ever, really—a disclosure that both horrified and fascinated her. One of the most photographed women in the world before the Kardashians flooded social media, and he didn't know who she was? Who would cut themselves off from the world like that? She felt drawn toward him now, determined to unravel the mystery.

"I'm Parith," she said, but he continued staring blankly. "Parith *Hilton.*"

"Hilton like the hotel?" the man asked. "Famous for being famous?"

She nodded.

"Good G-g-god, Paris Hilton is in my apartment," the man stammered, his face paling. "I d-didn't recognize you because of the tooth. Who sent you here?"

Her momentary joy at being recognized quickly faded. He didn't look like he wanted a picture or an autograph. Actually, her Paris glitter notwithstanding, he didn't even look *pleased* to have her in his apartment. He looked terrified. His face was completely white, his hands shaking, but soon enough, she would wear down his defenses. This was her gift: she could make others abandon their deepest convictions to experience a few more moments in her light, that beating life force and energy that effortlessly dripped off her like sweat, only she obviously never *actually* sweated.

She started explaining about the helicopter, her intention to land on the roof of the party, the importance of grand entrances. As for where the helicopter was now, she didn't know.

"So this was an accident?" he interrupted. "You d-don't know who I am? No one asked you to land here? No one's looking for you here?"

"I don't think tho."

"Well, that's a relief," said the man. He pulled out a notebook and began scribbling in cramped handwriting.

"Ith that your diary?" she asked, and he glared. "What are you writing?"

"I'm a writer. I write things."

"A reporter?" she asked hopefully.

"God no, not a reporter. A novelist. That helicopter story, that's good stuff. Would you mind telling me more?"

Thrilled as she was that he wanted to write about her, she shook her head. "Maybe thome other time. I have to get to my party. I jutht need a dentitht to make a houthe call here firtht. You thee," she pointed at the gap in her teeth. "I can't go out in public like thith. It would *ruin* me."

The man continued writing like he hadn't heard her, but when she began dialing her dentist, he yanked away her phone. She flinched, recalling the many boyfriends who'd stolen her electronics to read her private messages. "A *cell phone* in my apartment? You've got to be kidding me. I c-can't have *them* tracking me. No dentist house calls! No calls, period."

Before she could stop him, he ran outside and hurled the phone from the fire escape. She arrived just in time to watch it shatter in the gutter below. Clinging to the guardrail with her pink painted nails, she began sobbing. If she went out like this, some paparazzi would photograph her and destroy her comeback. She could already imagine the sneering headlines about her missing tooth: *Paris the Pirate. Hilton the Hockey Player.*

"Tom?" called a woman's voice from inside the apartment, muffled and hoarse. "Is everything OK out there?"

The old guy placed a gnarled hand on her shoulder. A warmth radiated down her spine. "I'm sorry about your phone," he said. "But we have to keep it down so my wife can sleep, and I can't have anyone following you up here. Maybe it's best if you get going, but I was hoping you could answer a few questions for me first. For my writing."

"You don't underthtand," she told him, sobbing even louder, ashamed that she was no longer being fun, that she had once more made herself unlovable. "I can't go out like thith or I'm *ruined*. I need my dentitht, and that phone wath my only way. Thath the only dentitht I know who makth emergenthy houthe callth thith late, and I only had hith number in my contacth. He'th not lithted."

She didn't explain the urgency, that her birthday good luck—the luck she'd need to show up Kim and reclaim her status—would wear out with the first rays of daylight.

Tom lifted his hand from her shoulder and began flipping through his notebook. In the moonlight, flecks of brown swam in his gray-green eyes, and he stroked his mustache, deep in thought. She knew this look, had seen it every so often with new tabloid reporters. That inner turmoil thing. A discomfort tangling with their hunger for the big scoop, a slight hesitation before snapping her photo.

"You know," Tom said, not lifting his eyes from the notebook, "I think I've g-got something that might work for both of us. A special dentist we can see right now. My wife can go back to sleep, and no one will see you in your current condition! I'll be right back."

Without waiting for her response, he went inside and disappeared into a back room. When she was sure he was gone, she wiped the remaining tears from her eyes, careful not to smudge her makeup. Who was this crazy old man, and how did he have access to such good emergency dental care? Also, who were the *They* he believed were tracking him? Paparazzi? What would paparazzi want with *him*?

Back inside the apartment, she searched for clues. This humble peasant dwelling reminded her of *The Simple Life*. Scuffed floors, exposed brick, bookshelves. Actually, now that she really looked, there were books everywhere. Books stacked in the corner and books spilling from sofa cushions. Books fanned across the coffee table. Books shoved horizontally in the gaps between bookshelves and books stuffed into empty cabinets. She picked up a few, then tossed them on the floor one by one like she was a child again, trying on her mother's perfumes in front of the armoire, humming her own invented melodies in the cavernous silence. Jasmine or lavender, orange blossom or coconut. And who would she be today?

She settled on a heavy hardback with a rocket ship on the cover, inhaling the earthy vanilla notes of the straw-tinged pages. So many long sentences, such small type. He'd said he was a writer. Had he written this?

She read the first sentence:

A screaming comes across the sky. It has happened before, but there is nothing to compare it to now.

"Life ith too thort for a long thtory," she muttered, flipping to the very last sentence in the book,

Now everybody—

So the lazy author hadn't even finished the sentence? She liked reading, but long books with lame endings like this were for nerds. Heiresses who didn't know how to have fun. Heiresses who didn't go on TV or start their own businesses. Heiresses who wore pearls, threw nice little tea parties with cucumber sandwiches, and cared too much whether other people thought they were "proper" heiresses: smart but not too smart, classy but not a bore, modest but still attractive. Being a proper heir was easy. You just slept with models and crashed yachts. But being a proper *heiress* was hard work. She'd never put up with it.

She lifted a second, shorter book and leafed through a few pages, pausing on a line underlined three times: *Shall I project a world?* Well, obviously. There was no point having money if you didn't spend it being yourself and projecting that self everywhere. Why be the same fake Prada purse hawked all up and down Canal Street when you could be a one-of-a-kind, brightly colored, *authentic* Louis Vuitton? For her entire adult life, from the moment she'd left that horrible boarding school for troubled teens, she'd tried channeling this authentic Louis Vuitton. To be a *true* heiress if not a proper one, much to her parents' disappointment. A true heiress followed her dreams and danced like no one was watching. A true heiress did not necessarily need money, though a good cash flow never hurt, and a true heiress had enough business savvy and street smarts to admit this. A true heiress was never boring. A true heiress helped others find and liberate their own true heiresses within. A true heiress revived her brand, rebuilt her empire, and projected her true inheritance—that fearlessly improper, one-of-a-kind, brightly colored, *authentic* Louis Vuitton self—across the globe. A true heiress never let anyone tell her who to be except her grandmother and only if that grandmother told her she was a star. She was hot. She never let anyone break her heart.

She dropped the book and moved on. In an adjacent room, she found a wooden desk teeming with blackened banana peels, Post-its with funny math equations, and hand-addressed envelopes marked with a strange horn symbol. On the corner of the desk sat a fourth-grader's sculpture: a long pink eraser with the pencil wire peeled off, a needle and paper clip threaded through to resemble a launching rocket. Next to this, a Porky Pig toy, a yo-yo, and a typewriter perched on a thick stack of graph paper covered with cramped handwriting.

She lifted one of the handwritten pages right as Tom walked in holding an umbrella. He'd changed into horrible ripped black jeans and stained red canvas sneakers. A faded plaid button-down opened over a black T-shirt for some band she didn't know, the Paranoids.

"Ith that really what you're wearing?" she asked.

"Why are you looking through my stuff?" he growled, snatching the graph paper from her hands. "That's *private*."

Her face flushed. She had said those same words to Rick, begging him not to release the full sex tape, her voice cracking on the long-distance call. It was a few years after she'd left the hell school. The thirty-seven second teaser had already begun circulating, threatening to shatter everything she'd built: her recently mended family relationships, the new career she had envisioned for herself as a respectable TV star, her recovering self-esteem. He had told her he was well within his rights to release the rest and then hung up, teaching her a lesson she'd never forget. It was horrible, but a fact of life, supply and demand or whatever: eventually, they'll find every last bit of your private soul and scrape it clean. Better to sell it to them instead.

"You're right," she said, lowering her eyes. "I'm thorry."

Tom smiled, baring his unfortunate teeth. "Well, I'm sorry too, because you're going to have to wear this so no one recognizes you. It would, to use your words, *ruin* you to be recognized with your teeth like this, right?" He handed her a brown lunch bag with holes punched for the eyes and mouth.

Was she really going through with this? Wrinkling her nose, she held the brown paper bag at arm's length and asked herself the eternal question: What would Marilyn do?

*

With some difficulty, his aging octogenarian joints not what they once were, Thomas Pynchon kneeled over the storm drain cover etched with the Trystero symbol. He set his umbrella on the pavement and ran his gnarled fingers along the rim until he found the right grooves. Then he dug in and lifted as gently as possible, his shaking hands momentarily smooth and controlled as he lowered the cast-iron lid to the street. He still couldn't believe he was returning underground after all these years, escorting a celebrity to a fictional dentist of all things just for some new writing material. New York, blasted city. This was the problem with living in the center of the big, stinking human mess when you weren't some show-off sellout like Mailer or Capote. You take all these measures to protect your privacy so you can write, and still, this sort of thing happens and then you have no choice but to go along with it because your wife's trying to sleep and already mad at you and because you have terrible writer's block and would give anything to write one more good novel before you die and because you can't help thinking maybe Paris is not just an It Girl but *it*, your last good idea, the one that'll finally win you the Pulitzer you were so rudely denied and who knows, maybe even the Nobel, and next thing you know, you're in the sewer. No choice no choice no choice. Salinger had the right idea, getting away to the country.

Climbing down the ladder, Tom took three deep breaths and exhaled, puffing out the brown paper lunch bag and warming his cheeks. Why had he been so terrified of this? Real outside air, nothing else like it. Even sewer stench smelled sweet, transported him back to those lazy sun-drenched Sunday afternoons the summer before he wrote his debut, drifting anonymously through the heatstroke city, the rotting garbage baking in the alleys, the curdling piles of human shit steaming in the subway tunnels, the stale piss park benches and the toilet water bodega coffee and the sticky spilled-beer sidewalks, everything sweat-stained and ashed with still-smoldering cigarette butts, and oh, how he missed it, yes, even that—that was how long he'd been cooped up, cut off, afraid to leave the apartment.

"What ith thith plathe?" Paris asked, after they'd both climbed down.

He shook off his umbrella and peeled back his paper bag. How to explain? It was the Zone, his mind's black market, the secret anarchist utopia he'd long prophesied where all his creations—at least, the ones who hadn't betrayed him—could run free. The Whole Sick Crew lived here, Benny Profane sometimes hunted his alligators, Pig Bodine and Kurt Mondaugen stopped by every so often, and of course Eigenvalue had also set up shop. He hadn't visited in so long.

"It's just a little place no one knows about b-but me— with a very good dentist. You've just got to watch out for the blind, albino gators," he said.

She smirked. "Ithn't that jutht an old wiveth tale?"

"No, they're real. Say, whaddya call an alligator in a vest?"

A blank stare. Blonde hair wisps fell into her eyes, and she tucked them behind her ears. He could tell she thought he was crazy, just a paranoid old man losing his grip on reality, but he also felt an unbelievable con-nection to her. In Paris's presence, he felt the same spark he experienced on his best writing days, so few and far between now, the words flowing through his fingertips, the pages effortless, everything possible again.

"An in*vesti*gator. Get it?"

She didn't laugh, and he was a little hurt by this but didn't let on. Silently, he led her to the door marked with the Trystero symbol and a small gold placard: *Dudley Eigenvalue, D.D.S., Soul Dentist.*

"After you," he said, pushing the door open. "Bear in mind, he's a t-tad *unconventional.*"

He followed Paris into the waiting room, which was just as he remembered. Hardback chairs with fluoride-colored fabric cushions, wilting potted plants in every corner, and an overpowering Windex and antibacterial soap smell. Horrible elevator music and Salvador Dali-inspired teeth paintings completed the picture. Only after his eyes adjusted to the new brightness did he notice the one addition: a dog was sitting in one of the chairs, reading a magazine. Could it be?

"Pugnax? Is that you?"

It had been ages. He hadn't seen Pugnax since the dog eloped with the talking pig from *GR*. The dog lowered the magazine, and now he realized his error. It was not his beloved Pugnax after all, just a scrawny Chihuahua wearing a pink sweater. His stomach sank. He hadn't realized just how badly he'd missed Pugnax, how badly he'd missed all his characters and friends.

"Sorry t-to disturb you," Tom stammered. "You just, you just looked so familiar a-and—"

A squeal interrupted his apology. Paris pushed past him, scooped up the little dog, and showered it with kisses. "Tinkerbell, oh Tink! Mummy mithed you thooo much!"

"Indeed," said the dog in a stilted, male British accent. "It is I, Tinkerbell the teacup Chihuahua, risen from the dead so we can both become famous again."

Tom's mouth fell open. He felt a sinking in his chest, a betrayal he hadn't expected to find here. This was supposed to be *his* sewer with *his* characters from *his* imagination. The night was growing stranger by the minute, and he didn't believe in coincidences. It was almost like They were rewriting his books, same as those early critics twisting his words to suit their petty agendas, his former friends twisting his personal life for their ten minutes of fame, reaching into his brain and rerouting the neural connections, searching for that one little part of himself, his very consciousness and essence, his Tom-ness, so they could snuff it out.

"Goodneth, Tink," Paris continued. "Mummy alwayth knew you were the thmartetht, bethtetht, motht beautifuletht dog ever, but even thee didn't realithe you could *talk* or turn into a boy."

"Yes, dear," the dog said disdainfully. "Reincarnation has changed me in some ways."

"Oh, Tink, I'm tho happy for you. We'll work for our dreamth together!" Paris hugged the Chihuahua tighter, and the small dog dropped his magazine, gasping for breath.

"Thee thith magathine?" said Paris, nudging Tom with her elbow. "If you're going to write about me—and you abtholutely thould—you thould make it more like the thtorieth in here. People like to read thomething fun and gothippy. Jutht nothing mean or I'll bury you."

Tom picked up the magazine, shocked to find his own face, fifty years younger, gazing back from the front cover. It was a black-and-white photo from college, before he'd met Richard, and seeing it now was painful. He had tried so hard to look ordinary in his conventional button-down and dark sports coat, his ink-black hair buzzed like a military recruit, but of course he had never fit in, not with his oversize ears and teeth, those caterpillar eyebrows. Richard had helped him finally understand this, had accepted him for who he was and shown him another way.

Above the photo, the headline in bold caps: HAVE YOU SEEN THIS AUTHOR? Below, a headshot of that actor with the funny name and hair lip dressed as Doc Sportello, all sideburns and aviator shades.

The Search for Thomas Pynchon:
Actor's Quest for Elusive Novelist Coming to Netflix
By Ian Scuffling

NEW YORK, NY. Netflix has announced a new television show based on Joaquin Phoenix's and Doc Sportello's search for the acclaimed yet reclusive novelist Thomas Pynchon.

The streaming service said it will debut the eight-episode series, *The Search for Thomas Pynchon*, later this summer. Filming for the pilot will begin immediately.

"We're so excited to partner with Joaquin and Doc to bring this exciting literary quest and ambitious performance project to a wider audience," said a Netflix spokesperson.

Last spring, the award-winning actor debuted an extended performance artwork in which he hired Doc Sportello, private investigator and protagonist of Thomas Pynchon's *Inherent Vice*, to locate the reclusive author. Phoenix, who played Sportello in the novel's 2014 film adaptation, has so far reprised that role for the duration of his performance.

"Now that Doc's found Shasta, it's time for Doc to find Thomas Pynchon. It's gonna be real groovy," said Phoenix as Sportello.

In addition to the two Sportellos, the show features an ensemble cast of literary sleuths from Pynchon's novels, including Herbert Stencil, Oedipa Maas, and Tyrone Slothrop. Each had hired Sportello independently prior to the show.

"Stencil wanted me to find V., Oedipa wanted me to find Trystero, and Slothrop wanted me to find the 00000 rocket. Since I wasn't having much luck finding those—major bummer—I convinced my clients we should all team up with Joaquin and try to find Pynchon instead," said Sportello as Sportello.

Winner of the 1974 National Book Award for *Gravity's Rainbow*, Thomas Pynchon has carefully avoided contact with the press for over fifty years, and his current whereabouts are unknown. Over the years, fans and critics alike have made numerous attempts to locate him, often circulating bizarre rumors about his "true" identity and his reasons for maintaining such strict privacy. (For a summary of these incidents, please see page 4.)

So Mel was wrong. The show had made it past pilot. Six months ago, when he first learned that Phoenix was pitching Netflix, he'd tried making Mel understand the very real threat this show posed to his privacy and ability to write, his very sense of self. She was sympathetic back then, brewing chamomile and rubbing his back in small circles, speaking softly. Most of these high-concept pitches failed before reaching pilot, she explained. It was probably just a publicity stunt that would blow over like all the others. No sense worrying about it at this early stage. But he *did* worry. He worried endlessly that They'd find him and that he'd consequently never break through his writer's block and if that happened, if he never felt the flow of words again, if he never felt that rush of possibility, if he never felt the world opening to the deepest parts of him, his very Tom-ness, then who even was he?

On the rare occasions he left the apartment after learning of Phoenix's pitch, he'd swear he saw Sportello exiting a cab or Oedipa standing in line at the grocery. The sightings left him dizzy and nauseated, unable to speak for hours, nearly suicidal. Eventually, he stopped leaving the apartment entirely. Transitioned from regular recluse to paranoid delusional recluse. Ignored lunch invitations from DeLillo, Rushdie, McEwan until they stopped calling. Tossed the television and phones. Slept with a gun. He was sure They were trying to find him and that, once They did, They'd destroy his freedom, corrupt his work, sell him to the media for a quick buck. The equation was simple:

(famous actor + reclusive writer) x 50 years
of silence = tabloid story of a lifetime =
$$\$$$

At first, Mel and Jack had accommodated his new paranoias. Mel left her cell phone at the office, and Jack visited more often from Brooklyn. Then three months ago, everything had changed when Jack's band was invited to play at a music hall in Williamsburg, a huge step up from their usual dive bars. On learning the news, Jack had ridden the subway up from Bushwick to tell his parents in person.

"This is *it*," Jack had announced, running a hand through his shaggy black hair, cheeks flush from racing up the stairs. "Our big break. You'll both be there, right?"

Tom had stared into his son's eyes, carbon copies of his own but brighter, less jaded. He remembered himself at this age, so naïve and hopeful, writing in Mexican coffee shops and smoking dope, his literary ambitions still untarnished by the *Time* reporter chasing him or the Pulitzer board's hurtful description of *GR*. It was good that Jack had dreams, good for him to work toward something.

"Of course," he said. "I wouldn't miss it for the world."

He'd fully intended to keep his word. But when the evening of the concert arrived, he hesitated. After months of caution, why take such a big risk? Why throw it all away? What if They were at the concert? What if They were behind the whole thing, using the son to find the father? Surely, Jack would understand. His son would have other concerts once this Netflix threat was over.

He and Mel had already changed into their black Paranoids T-shirts when he told her he couldn't go. Gently but firmly, she reminded Tom of all she and Jack had given up for his privacy and his writing and not just during these last few months of worsening paranoia.

"Remember when Jack had to transfer from Vassar because of the attention? To take down his Facebook page? Not to mention all those stalker photos of him as a child."

His chest tightened. He remembered walking Jack home from school that day, his hand curled tightly around his seven-year-old's sticky little fingers, when the photographer leaped out and took their photo. He had never felt so helpless as a parent, so unable to protect his own son.

"All these years," Mel continued, "and no complaints, none, because he loves you. And all he wants in return is for you to love him back and be there for him. I know it wasn't your decision to be famous or to have the press treat you this way, and I respect your decision not to be a public figure, to focus on your art. You know that. But you have a *choice* now. Are you going to be there for your son?"

"You know I want to," he said, his voice breaking. "But…"

"But what?" Mel snapped. "What's more important than this?"

"B-but what if it's…Them?"

Mel had gathered her purse and stormed out. For the next half hour, he'd stood in the doorway, trying to make himself follow her.

Now, months later, he was ashamed. Why would he follow Paris from the apartment but not his own wife and son? Why would he risk himself for his writing but not for the people he loved? He folded the article and shoved it in his back pocket so he could show Mel and Jack later. Maybe it would help them understand that he'd been right to worry and to avoid Jack's concert because he'd had no choice no choice no choice. Maybe it would help them forgive him.

"Tom!" shouted Eigenvalue, sticking his fat head through the receptionist's window at last. "Long time, no see. What brings you in today, and who's your lovely friend with the dog?"

Paris's mouth fell open. "Theriouthly? You don't know who I am either?"

"Paris, you'll have to forgive Eigenvalue here. He lives in the sewer so he doesn't know much about celebrities," said Tom.

The dentist smiled sheepishly.

"Eigenvalue, you have no idea how good it is to see you," Tom continued, beaming. He could still remember when the dentist was only a rough character sketch, just a few lines of dialogue Tom had patiently and lovingly shaped into a complete character with his own desires and fears. "This is Paris. She knocked a tooth out and needs it fixed right away so she can get to a party."

"So *we* can get to a party," added Tinkerbell.

Paris smiled, and Eigenvalue bent closer to examine the gap in her teeth.

"Oh my, well, we'll certainly fix that right up! And I'm assuming the dog's just here for a standard canine tooth brushing?" The Chihuahua nodded. "All right then, come along!"

They followed the dentist down a long hallway to an exam room more Freudian than clinical, all fluffy pillows, dusty bookshelves, and sage. Hidden speakers piped in cascading water sounds. Worn pillows and an ornate geometric rug draped a long Victorian-style bed in the middle of the room.

Tom took the velvet armchair in the corner. Eigenvalue directed Paris to the daybed, and Tinkerbell hopped into her lap.

"Now, Paris," Eigenvalue said, laying a steno pad across his knee and uncapping a ballpoint pen. "Before we get started with healing your tooth, I want to address your soul. Your psyche. Anything on your mind today?"

She shook her head and continued scratching the Chihuahua's ears. "I jutht want my tooth fixed tho I can be hot again."

"Hmm, I see." Eigenvalue scribbled on his pad a few notes that Tom couldn't decipher. "And what does that mean to you, being hot? Why's being hot so important to you?"

"I like feeling hot. It makth me feel good when everyone lookth at me and wanth to be with me or to be my betht friend and knowth my name. I want to be famouth again."

"Fame, hmm, I see."

As the dentist scribbled more notes, Tom rolled his eyes and suppressed a groan. Paris so willingly gave herself to Them. Like Mucho Maas on LSD, merged with the masses, all individuality smothered. Like Slothrop, conditioned to ejaculate on command, a drooling Pavlovian dog beholden to cause and effect. He thought of his brother and sister, perfect miniatures of his parents, who were themselves replicas of the neighbors, everyone living in identical houses with identical dreams, everyone driving their miniatures to identical schools, where all the children wore uniforms and taunted him for his teeth and stutter, their laughs all sounding the same, as though they had fused into

one many-headed monster. Was there any part of Paris
They hadn't touched yet? A Paris They hadn't used?

He pulled out his notebook and jotted down an equation:

$$Paris - (conditioned\ Paris) = who?$$

Eigenvalue continued, "And how do you feel when
you're not famous?"

"Like I, like I don't even exitht. If no one theeth you,
you're nothing."

"So who are you now then, if you don't exist?"

This time, no response. Tom couldn't imagine what she
might be thinking, but she was clearly bothered. Her face
froze, and she even stopped petting the dog. So he was
wrong, she had her private griefs. They all did, didn't they?

$$Paris - (conditioned\ Paris) = \sout{who?}\ private$$
$$griefs + ?$$

As he wrote, he thought of Marilyn Monroe's death and
how it had shaken him. Years later, and it still didn't make
sense. To be *so loved*. To have so much. To still feel so much
pain. He'd said it then, and he'd say it again: if the world
couldn't make those private griefs bearable, the world was
at fault. Maybe he'd been too harsh on Paris. Maybe there
was more to her than met the eye.

The dentist yawned. "You don't need to answer,
of course. If you knew all the answers, you wouldn't have
much need for me, now would you? Here, let me show you
a little something about your teeth." Eigenvalue handed
Paris a mirror and prodded her teeth with his pen. "You

see your tooth there and the little pulp bit where it fell out? That soft and squishy pulp there is actually your *id*. Your unconscious self. It's the hard, outer enamel that fell off, and that enamel is your *superego*, responsible for your critical and moral decisions. That enamel right there—*that's* what we're going to replace!" He paused for a moment to let this sink in. Cheerily, he continued, "You'll be the same person inside, you see, with the same instinctual desires for fame and so forth, but the super-ego will be different now, and so will your morality and decision-making process."

"Um, excuthe me?"

Before Paris could ask more questions, the dentist slapped an anesthesia mask on her. Paris's body slackened, relaxing into the chair's curve. Her arms loosened around the dog, and her eyes blinked closed. Tom leaned forward.

"That last part always freaks 'em out," said the dentist, addressing Tom now. "It's like they think they have free will or something. What does it matter whether it's one super-ego or the other, eh?"

Tom crossed his arms. He disagreed with the dentist about free will. There were still choices and gaps in Their conditioning. Nodes. A sigh in the gravity, a quirk in the psychology, a break in the wars, a blackness between the frames that no rational machine or economy could condition.

"Now normally, I'd prefer an implant here, but that requires a bone graft so we'll do a bridge instead. You know what a bridge is, Tom?"

He shook his head no, feeling foolish.

"A bridge looks like three teeth but is really just the two real teeth sandwiched around a fake tooth and fused together into one object. It's a linear illusion, nothing more. To put it in terms you'll understand, think of the real teeth as historical events. You've got a past event here and a future event there, not really connected by anything *real*, of course, but they appear that way. The rational human mind perceives events as linear and connected even when there's no chain of cause or effect. That damn rocket of yours, eh?" He winked, jabbing himself in the chest. "But me, I'm a soul-dentist, not a dentist-historian or dentist-philosopher—required too much postgrad, if you want the truth. Anyway, as a *soul-dentist*, I view each tooth as representing an aspect of the past or future self. As with your history, there's still the cause and effect illusion with the self. Past and future selves appear more connected than they really are because, if you'll notice, even the most perfect smile has little gaps between the teeth."

$$\text{past event} \rightarrow \text{future event}$$
$$\text{past Paris} \rightarrow \text{future Paris}$$
$$\text{past Paris} \quad \text{future Paris}$$

"That's what floss is for, making sure those gaps don't fill with anything else, anything that might interfere. You're remembering to floss, right?"

Tom nodded. He hadn't flossed in months and was eager to change the subject. "So what does that mean when you introduce a fake tooth?"

"Ah, an excellent question! It means a bigger gap. A real chance to deviate from a strictly linear path of desires! Our

friend Paris here might just do something tonight that surprises you, something out of character."

past Paris 〔ᗢ〕〔ᗢ〕〔ᗢ〕 *future Paris*

Eigenvalue winked and slapped his palms on his knees.
"But enough psychology. On with the dentistry!" The exam
room soon filled with the dental drill's high-pitched, grat-
ing scream.

Plugging his ears, Tom pulled out his magazine and
flipped to the article on page 4.

The Search for Thomas Pynchon: Rumors and Sightings
By Ian Scuffling

NEW YORK, NY. Little is known about Thomas Pynchon,
an author so reclusive he sent a comedian to accept his
1974 National Book Award. Since 1963, when Pynchon fled
a *Time* magazine reporter in Mexico and disappeared from
public life, colorful rumors about his identity and the reasons for his closely-guarded privacy have proliferated.

In the 1970s, a *Soho Weekly* article argued that Pynchon
was actually the pseudonym of another reclusive author: J. D.
Salinger. Separately, a *Playboy* article by a former classmate
alleged Pynchon had an affair with the classmate's wife and
hid from shame. Others have speculated that Pynchon is Ted
Kaczynski, a Waco Branch Davidian sympathizer, or "Wanda
Tinasky," the cranky pseudonymous author of numerous let-
ters to the editor in the late 1980s. Still, others claim Pynchon
is hiding from the CIA, ashamed of his infamous buckteeth,
or brain-damaged from an LSD overdose.

These rumors have only further motivated devoted fans and curious reporters to unravel the mystery. In 1997, a CNN camera crew filmed Pynchon near his Manhattan home but did not identify him to viewers in the footage. The following year, a *Sunday Times* reporter photographed Pynchon walking with his son.

Others criticize this obsession, favoring a simpler explanation for Pynchon's reclusiveness. "The man simply chooses not to be a public figure, an attitude that resonates on a frequency so out of phase with that of the prevailing culture that if Pynchon and Paris Hilton were ever to meet—the circumstances, I admit, are beyond imagining—the resulting matter/antimatter explosion would vaporize everything from here to Tau Ceti IV," book critic Arthur Salm wrote in the *San Diego Union-Tribune* in 2004.

That same year, in a possible sign of shifting winds, Pynchon broadcast his voice to a major media outlet for the first time, appearing on *The Simpsons* as an animated cameo character. (In a nod to Pynchon's anonymity, the character wore a paper lunch bag over his head.) More recently, Pynchon's voice was recorded in a promotional YouTube teaser for his novel, *Inherent Vice*. As to what the man is up to these days and whether he's really warming to the press, who can say?

Tom closed the magazine, disgusted. Did they really think he was warming to the press? After fifty years of careful avoidance, after everything he'd given up, everything Mel and Jack had suffered, the mere suggestion offended him. But that was just like the press. They were so smallminded. They saw what they wanted, ignored the reality, had no imagination. That line about him and Paris meeting said it all: *If Pynchon and Paris Hilton were ever to meet...circumstances beyond imagining.* Clearly not!

He returned to his notebook. Already, the novel's basic plot was forming. Another journey perpetually deferred, another doomed quest for the grail, another detective martyred to capitalism and celebrity culture. He'd hardly have to invent anything this time, just incorporate the real details Paris was already feeding him and embellish some. The doomed quest was to upstage another celebrity, the grail was Kim Kardashian herself, and those fans who mindlessly consumed such drivel were no better than the bureaucrat-engineers who mindlessly built the Rocket. Teeth and talking dogs, nice additions as always. And the crash helicopter landing would remind readers of *GR*.

> *grail = Kim*
> *detective = Paris*
> *fans = engineers*
> *helicopter = rocket = V2 =*
> *SEXUAL LOVE OF DEATH DRIVE*

Tom closed his notebook right as Eigenvalue turned off the drill and began brushing the dog's teeth. A soft scratching, his nostrils filling with mint. A few minutes later, Paris woke up, and the dentist handed her a mirror.

"Oh thank you, Dr. Dudley! Thank you so much. They're *perfect*." She turned slightly to examine the teeth from a new angle. "Loves it, loves it."

Tom stared at her new teeth. They were white and flawless, not even a hint of chipping or discoloration. The same teeth he'd seen in countless toothpaste ads. The same teeth everyone else had and that Mel had so desperately wanted. A year ago, he'd found bleach whitening strips in the bathroom. "For the coffee stains," Mel had explained, and he'd burst into tears. He told her he loved her teeth—they were hers, they were perfect. Why would she ever alter them? Obviously she could make decisions about her own body and he'd support her choices, but he just didn't understand why this was necessary. The next day, when he found the strips in the trash, he'd felt guilt and relief all at once.

The dentist beamed. "May they serve you well. How's about we hear that catchphrase of yours without the lisp?"

"That's hot."

Hearing Paris say these words, Tom felt like he was back in the bathroom with Mel, crying over the whitening strips. He hadn't realized how much he'd loved Paris's lisp, how much he'd identified with it because of his own stutter. He leaned back in the chair and dug his nails into his temples, mourning the lost black gap. Then he pulled out his notebook again and began writing:

> *journey of perpetual deferment = gradual hollowing out of self?*
>
> *Valley girl "like" = gap in speech =* 🦷 *= chance to deviate = node???*

"Marvelous, marvelous. You're all set. Now, Tom," said Eigenvalue, swiveling his chair around. "If you'd like, I can fix yours, too."

Heat rose in Tom's cheeks, and his heart beat madly. The dentist had never suggested this before. After everything he'd just heard about the psychological effects of Eigenvalue's procedures, he could not help but view the offer as a threat: Eigenvalue wanted to fix his teeth to alter *Tom's mind*. To destroy his Tom-ness. Did this mean the dentist was working for Them, trying to pacify Tom for an easy Netflix delivery? Had Eigenvalue betrayed him and crossed over to the dark side just to make a quick buck? No, it couldn't be. He must not be seeing clearly. "That's really OK, b-but—"

"You think They're after you again, don't you?" Eigenvalue interrupted. His fat face was friendly and damp with sweat, but something sinister lurked behind the eyes. A digital clock face, a negatively charged ion, a parabola-shaped deathliness. Where was his essence, the Eigenvalue-ness that Tom had given him back when he was but a wee character sketch? Had They snuffed it out? "Look, Tom, I'm your friend and want to help. Some good psycho-dentistry might do wonders. Make you blend in more, relieve the paranoia…"

Well, if that didn't just *prove* Eigenvalue was working for Them! Tom swallowed hard, terrified but also deeply hurt. Eigenvalue, one of his oldest and most beloved characters, was now just as corrupted as the detectives. Did this mean his other characters would soon betray him too, leaving him all alone? Thinking of Oedipa and Pugnax, his eyes filled with tears, and he blinked them away. Slowly but forcefully, he shook his head. *No, sir. You will not operate on my soul, you will not tell Them where I am or make me useful*

*or fit me into your rational death march. You will not make
me like everyone else.*

He picked up his umbrella and motioned for Paris and
the dog to follow him to the waiting room. Standing in the
doorway, he threw his former creation—poor, luckless
pawn in Their scheme—one last, long, sorrowful look.
"A pun for you, Doc. What did the d-dentist say to the
saber-toothed tiger?"

They left before Eigenvalue could respond.

*

Back in the sewer, Paris stood on her tiptoes to admire her
reflection in a large, rusted pipe. What a great tooth, even
better than before. The night now seemed full of possibility. Because of what the dentist had said about her super-
ego? She licked the tooth with the tip of her tongue, the
dentist's words echoing in her mind like an annoying pop
song on repeat, not one of hers. *You'll still be the same person
inside, you see, with the same instinctual desires for fame and
so forth, but the superego will be different now, and so will your
morality and decision-making process... It's like they think they
have free will or something. What does it matter whether it's one
superego or the other, eh?*

All that mumbo jumbo about morality and free will had
reminded her of Sunday school, giggling beside Nicky
while a sharp-faced nun in a hideous black frock lectured
from the catechism, "To God, all moments of time are present in their immediacy. When therefore he establishes his
eternal plan of predestination, he includes in it each person's free response to his grace."

As a child, she'd been like the dentist. She hadn't understood how a person could be free much less *be* a person in any meaningful way when God already knew how their story would end, knew the last line of their book. It reminded her of high school physics, the little she had learned before she was sent away, the incompatibility of general relativity and quantum mechanics. Big Physics and Little Physics. Only years later, after her anger at God had temporarily cooled, did it make more sense. Her own personal Theory of Strings or whatever. On a large scale, on the level of history, everything was planned and orderly. On a small scale, on the level of each individual human, there was choice and randomness, and this chaos was more meaningful because of the orderliness. The large scale allowed for the small scale, a limited but more meaningful freedom. Luther, paraphrasing Augustine, had said it better, "Free will without grace has the power to do nothing but sin." Grace allowed for a wider range of freedoms just like her birthday luck allowed for a little extra magic tonight just like this new tooth allowed for a night full of new possibilities. To Augustine's words, she had written her own addendum, about a different kind of grace: "Grace without beauty is worthless."

And wasn't this what the dentist had given her? Grace and a wider range of choices because now she had beautiful teeth again, and beautiful people could do anything.

Tinkerbell nudged Paris's ankle. "My dear, I hate to interrupt your self-admiration, but we really should get to our party and allow this gentleman," he pointed a paw at Tom, who was scribbling in his notebook again, "to take leave. After all, we only have a few more hours until your birthday magic wears off."

Paris turned away from the pipe and picked up Tinkerbell. How had she gone all these years without her best friend, the only one who had never let her down? Tink was right, they had work to do. Together, they would take on Kim, reinvigorate her brand, rebuild her empire. They would conquer social media and win back all her old fans, the Little Hiltons who would shower her once more with praise and adoration. "OK, Tink," she whispered. "You know how to get us there once we're out of the sewer?"

Tinkerbell perked his ears. "Do *I* know how to get there?"

"To the party. To Kim."

"My dear, you do realize I'm a dog, don't you? I once spent a whole day chasing my tail, I defecate outside, and now you expect *me* to navigate?"

She stared at the shimmering pink toes poking from her sparkling silver pumps, her cheeks hot. Here she was again, falling into the dumb blonde stereotype she was still fighting despite all her boss bitch success with her company. "I actually don't know where the club is," she muttered.

Tinkerbell looked at her with renewed disgust, his pink tongue rolling from his mouth.

"You don't know where it is?" Tom asked gently.

"I've always had a driver," she explained, reminding Tom that he'd destroyed her phone with the maps and that she'd also lost her purse and wallet when she fell from the helicopter. She couldn't even hail a cab now. "All I know is the name. The Sailor's Grave."

"The Sailor's Grave," Tom repeated, stunned. "I know that place. There's actually a special entrance here underground. It's that way," he pointed his umbrella down a tunnel to their left. "I could take you there if you'd like."

"Really?" How could someone dressed so terribly know about a cool new club?

"*Really*," said Tom.

"I'd be very grateful for your help," she said, flashing her new smile. "And you haven't finished writing about me yet."

"Why of course," he said, flipping to a fresh page in his notebook. "My pleasure."

For well over a mile, she followed Tom through the dark tunnel, her pumps clattering against the wet stone, until her feet finally began to hurt. "Hey, how far did you say it was?" she asked Tom. "I didn't exactly wear my walking shoes."

"Not much farther at all, but we can take a break if you like."

"Yes, pleeeeeease," she said, bending to remove her shoe as Tom looked on, amused. "Hey, what are you laughing at? You men have no idea how—"

A sharp, distant hissing drowned out her words. She straightened up. Tom was staring down the tunnel, eyes wide and alert. Tinkerbell's tail was raised, his ears perked.

"What was that?" she asked.

A deep, guttural bellowing echoed down the long tunnel.

Without answering, Tom seized her arm and dragged her to the tunnel's side, toward a large bronze pipe, maybe four feet in diameter and two feet off the ground, jutting from the wall.

"Hey, what the hell, get off me!" she shouted, struggling to free her arm from his tight grip, her earlier panic returning.

"Shh, quiet!" Tom whispered. "It's g-got excellent hearing."

"What's got excellent hearing?"

He shoved her into the opening, pushing her head down so she wouldn't hit it on the low ceiling. The rotten eggs smell was overpowering. She coughed and held her nose, stepping gingerly around the stagnant water pooled in the pipe's center. The pipe was not very long, dead-ending a few feet ahead of her and curving upward.

"We'll be safe in here," Tom whispered, crawling in after her with Tinkerbell.

"Safe from what?" she asked.

"From the b-blind, albino gators. Remember?"

Surely, he was joking? She inched over to make room for them, crouching in the pipe's curve, Tink trembling at her feet, the awful growling and hissing growing louder. She looked up. Overhead, a metal grate covered pure darkness, as if she had fallen into a black hole where no light, no energy, could ever escape. She hugged her knees to her chest, the awful memory bubbling to the surface again, slipping through her fingers despite her best efforts to drown it. All at once, she was back at the hell school again, back in the cramped, cinder-block chamber with feces-smeared walls where they locked her after she was caught spitting out the mind-numbing pills. She could still hear the male staffers laughing as they stripped her clothes away, could still feel her naked body shivering beside the damp toilet paper roll and reeking piss bucket.

"I have to get out of here," she blurted out, blinking back tears. "Whatever's making those noises can't be worse than *this*."

"Fool!" snarled Tinkerbell, blocking her path. "Stay put! I didn't go to the most exclusive groomer in the sewer this morning to wind up *hors d'oeuvres du lézard!*"

She brushed Tink aside and crawled toward the opening, elbowing Tom in the stomach when he tried to stop her. Grunting, he doubled over. She pushed past him.

Another roar, much closer this time, rumbled against the tunnel's walls. Tink whimpered from behind her, tail tucked between his legs. She looked out from the pipe in the direction of the noise and could now make out a pale form, long and low to the ground, emerging from the tunnel's darkness. As whatever it was crawled along the wet stones, she realized it was a large, scaly creature of some sort with a tapered head, thick tail, and stumpy Keira Knightley legs. Creepiest of all was the thing's coloring. It was completely white, its spikes and scales like those intricate limestone carving thingies from her trip to Greece. Even its eyes were white, milky and unseeing, colorless except for the slitted red pupils, like some totally disgusting sea monster. A blind, albino alligator just like Tom had said!

She gasped. The alligator swiveled its long head in their direction and sniffed. Paris held her breath, her heart frozen in her chest. A moment later, the massive reptile was upon her, hissing and gurgling and thrashing, biting at the air and trying to get at her like some super aggressive paparazzi. She removed her sparkly pumps and flung them down, aiming for the creature's icky eyes, but this only majorly PO'd it. The giant lizard let out a deep, groaning roar, then hurled its slimy upper body into the pipe. A gust of hot breath, completely gross and fishy, then a flash of yucky, yellowing teeth that made her want to vom.

She screamed. Tom yanked her back and smacked the alligator's broad snout with his closed umbrella. The reptile faltered like a drunk party girl in ten-inch heels, then recovered, lurching forward. Tom swung again, but that bitch was ready this time, knocking the umbrella aside with ease. The umbrella clattered against the wall of the pipe, snapping open. The reptile hissed, shredding the umbrella's canopy with its claws. Tom tripped, stumbling backward. She tried reaching for him but couldn't move her arms. Her body tingled, then went numb. As the gator bore down, Tom covered her with his body. She tried screaming again, but the sound died trapped in her throat.

Instead, she heard the sharp, deafening crack of what sounded like shitty fireworks—so loud it shook her whole body and knocked the breath out of her—and then the softer, echoing thud of the stupid creature's heavy body crumpling against the bottom of the pipe. A nasty burning smell, like triply rotted eggs mixed with metal, filled her nostrils. A high-pitched whistling rang in her ears.

"Sorry for the delay," said a nasally male voice. She felt Tom loosening his embrace, the weight lifting. She looked around him and saw a chubby, beady-eyed, baby-faced man kneeling over the dead alligator. "You two OK?" Baby Face asked, slinging his rifle back over his shoulder.

"Benny, you *schlemiel*," Tom gasped. "We were nearly k-killed."

Baby Face shrugged, fiddling with his rifle strap. "Well, I gotta run. There's a whole pack of 'em headed to Eigenvalue. Later gators," he said, saluting them on his way out.

Tom stood and handed Paris back her shoes. As she put them back on, Tom bent to examine his ruined umbrella, then tossed it aside. He offered her his hand. She took it—not because she wanted to after the way he'd dragged and shoved her, but because she was still unsteady—and stepped shakily to her feet, gazing warily at the alligator. Its white scales would look great on a little clutch purse.

"It's really dead?" she asked.

"Yes, very dead," said Tom.

They stepped around the motionless form and back into the main tunnel, blinking in the dim lights. Tink raised a leg, relieving himself on the tunnel wall. She looked away. Her chest was still pounding, her hands clammy and cold. She took several long, slow breaths like the therapy chick had taught her and reminded herself that she was in a safe space and in control of her body. The men who had dragged her away in the night, the men who had laughed at her naked body, locked her in solitary, and taunted her endlessly, calling her names and telling her she was unworthy of love—they were not here. They could not still hurt her. On her next exhale, she felt the awful memory slipping back beneath the surface, sinking away.

"Everything all right?" asked Tom.

She nodded, slowly returning to the present.

"I'm really sorry about the gator. I'll have to give Benny a p-piece of my mind next time I see him, make sure he's not working for Them. It gave you quite a fright, huh?"

"Yes, no. It's not the gator. I don't like being in confined spaces. Feeling trapped."

Tom's expression softened, but he looked confused.

"I was locked up this one time, as a teenager," she added.

"Juvie?" he asked, his eyes full of pity.

She blushed, already regretting her words. The way he was looking at her now, like some wounded baby bird fallen from the nest, was completely cringe.

"No, not juvie. Just some dumb boarding school. It's nothing really." She laughed a little so he'd believe her, but the lines around his brows only hardened.

"Doesn't sound like n-nothing."

She swallowed hard. In moments like this, it was best to change the subject. "Back there," she asked, gesturing in the direction of Eigenvalue's office, "why wouldn't you let the dentist fix your teeth?"

He stared like he didn't understand the question. Like *he* was a dumb blond. "Something wrong with my teeth?"

She adjusted her tiara and avoided Tom's eyes, unable to tell him the truth. His teeth were terrible. No one who mattered had teeth like that.

"Well..."

"They're *my* teeth," Tom protested.

"And you don't care at all what other people think, my good sir?" asked Tinkerbell.

Tom shot them both a disgusted look, shoving his gnarled hands into his hideously ripped jeans. He thought he was so much better than her and Tink with his snobby books and his ugly clothes, but he wasn't! They just dealt in different currencies. She projected her image and he his words. No way he didn't care what people *thought* of those words.

"I d-don't. I don't care at all."

"Like that's true," Paris scoffed, half-surprised to hear the words tumbling from her mouth. "Everyone cares what others think."

"Why do *you* care?" Tom asked. "Why do you care so much about being famous and getting to this party? Why do you play a d-dumb character of yourself for the cameras?"

Paris flicked some dirt from her nails. Who'd he think he was talking to her like that? After everything she'd accomplished and all the indignities she'd suffered, after letting him write about her, which would probably boost his career, he had *some nerve*. "You think there were other roles for me to play?" she snapped. "I was only a teenager when I started acting and had just left that terrible school. The producers wanted me to play a dumb blonde, so I did. I really would've done like, anything they asked."

Tom snorted. "That's pathetic."

"You're pathetic," Tink growled.

"You have no idea what it was like for me at that school," she shouted, thumping her chest. "They told me I was a lazy, stupid nobody, a worthless piece of shit whose family was better off without me. And you know how I got through that? I told myself that one day I'd become so successful—so fabulously, disgustingly rich and famous—that no one could ever say those things to me again. That show was going to be my big break."

"Fine, fine," Tom said. "I g-get why you started playing this character. But why did you keep going with it? You're not a teenager anymore. You could've stopped."

She rolled her eyes. "Yeah, but by then I was *Paris Hilton*. The audience loved me, the press loved me."

"Loved you? They took *advantage* of you."

She chuckled. "Only at first. The producers, the paparazzi, Rick—they all took advantage of me initially. But when life handed me lemons, I decided to make the best, booziest damn lemonade this world has ever tasted."

"That's right, dear," Tink nodded approvingly. "The best except for Beyoncé's."

"I worked the character to my own advantage. Made a name for myself. Launched my career."

There, it was out. She'd confessed her hypocrisy. Tink rubbed up against her leg, and she patted his head. When this was all over, she'd paint his nails pink, buy him all new treats, spoil him rotten. Another Furcedes and Swarovski crystal-covered leash, a pink and white Fifi & Romeo coat, maybe even a new ferret friend or exotic monkey. That was all she wanted sometimes, to take care of Tink and her other animals. She cleared her throat. "Hardly anyone knows this," she said, turning to Tom. "But when I was little, I wanted to be a veterinarian. I've always loved animals and figured it couldn't be half bad, taking care of creatures who love us so unconditionally, who make us feel less lonely."

Tom looked stunned. "But you didn't become a veterinarian."

She shook her head. "You know how your dog looks at you when you first walk in? I had *whole rooms* of people looking at me like that. Whole rooms of people looking at me like that for years and years, and I thought, *Now I'll never be lonely again.* I realized I could do something for these people. I could act out in ways they weren't allowed. I could help them find that inner confidence, be their own heiresses." She sighed, shaking her head. "Then eventually they all moved on. It happened so quickly. Like I woke up one day, and the Kardashians were everywhere. No one cared about me anymore. It was like I was right back where I started, wondering whether anyone would ever love me again."

Tom placed a warm hand on her shoulder, a basic kindness in his eyes like Gram's, and wasn't that all she needed? Besides Tinkerbell, none of her best friends or thirty-five pets—even after two seasons and two international spin-offs of *Paris Hilton's My New BFF*, even after producers in Germany, Russia, Italy, and Japan begged her to keep searching for BFFs around the world—had shown her this basic kindness. "I'm sure people care about you," he said. "You know, I made a decision like that once when I was very young. Something that altered the whole course of my life."

She wiped her eyes. "You did?"

He told her some crazy, made-up story about fleeing paparazzi in Mexico and then going into hiding. "The more I retreated, the more they made of me, and so I had to hide even more. Now I hardly know anyone. B-barely leave the house."

She resisted the urge to call him a liar. What a nutter. He was even kookier than she'd realized—fancied himself on *her* level, a celebrity with adoring fans— but a true heiress was nice to loonies like that. Just because it wasn't real didn't mean he wasn't really suffering. Rule number seven: *Always tell people what they want to hear.*

"Tom, that's one of the saddest things I've ever heard." Clasping his hand in hers, she began singing from her album to cheer him up. To her surprise, he joined in at the chorus, following it with a stanza of his own:

> And all the world's busy, this twi-light!
> Who knows what morning-streets, our shoes have known?
> Who knows, how many friends, we've left, to cry alone?
> We have a moment together,
> We'll hum this tune for a day . . .
> Ev'ryone's dancing, in twi-light,
> Dancing the bad dream a-way . . .

"I didn't know you wrote music," she said, when he finished. "That was beautiful."

"It's nothing," he said, blushing.

"No, don't discount yourself. It really was very good."

For a moment, he looked like he was about to cry. She wondered when he'd last received a compliment like this or shared his crazy story with a sympathetic listener.

"That's very kind of you," he said softly. "We should really get going though, shouldn't we? Get you to your club?"

She nodded solemnly, and they resumed their trek. After what felt like forever, they finally arrived at yet another door marked with that weird gold horn symbol and a tiny gold placard: *The Sailor's Grave.*

Inside, the club was unlike any she'd ever seen, a hideous mess of rickety, wooden tables, garish posters, clouded chandeliers, and melting candles. Bizarrely, the club was also completely silent. No music, no speaking, and certainly no Kim. Dust coated the scuffed wooden floor, and her nostrils filled with cheap cigarette smoke. Behind the wooden bar, potbellied men in white sailor uniforms crouched over beer nozzles shaped like sad, sagging boobs and gestured in sign language while pockmarked waitresses with unfortunate bangs and identical plastic name tags (Beatrice) swooped between tables, lifting fogged glasses and wiping spills. What was this, unsexy Halloween?

"What's going on?" she asked. "Why's there no music?"

Tink pointed to the bright posters striping the walls, each with that same weird horn symbol again. So they were all connected. "My dear, they have a weekly schedule right here. Monday is a meeting of the Peter Pinguid Society, Wednesday a Paranoids concert, Friday a support group for Inamorati Anonymous, Sunday a colonial America trivia game, and all other nights, including tonight, is the Deaf-Mute Sailor's Silent Rave."

"The *what?*" she asked, turning to Tom.

"I don't know what to tell you," he said, apologetic. "You saw the sign on the d-door. You sure your club was called the Sailor's Grave?"

She bit her lip. Maybe there were two Sailor's Graves or maybe she had the name wrong. Well, didn't that just figure with the night she was having? At this rate, she'd never get to the right club and upstage Kim. "Come on, Tink," she said. "We should leave so we can find Kim before it's too late, and all my birthday magic's gone." She scooped up the dog and turned to exit right as a heavy disco ball plunged from the ceiling, nearly smacking her in the head. Instinctively, she covered her new tooth and stepped backward. Strobe lights and LEDs were now blinking from the walls, and the sailors were wiping their drooling mouths on their sleeves, belching loudly, stumbling red-faced to the dance floor.

"Looks like they're about to start the silent rave," said Tom. "I know you're in a rush to find Kim, but we have no idea where she might be. We're already here. Why don't we stay for a song or two?"

She was about to say no when she felt like like like a strange tingling sensation in her tooth. A vibrating warmth from the inside out, like finding the perfect outfit. With the tip of her tongue, she traced the smooth enamel and reconsidered. Would it really matter if she were a little late to the club? Her eyes settled on a clock in the corner. She still had a few more hours before her birthday magic wore off, plenty of time.

"I guess we can stay for a song or two," she said, lowering Tinkerbell to the ground. She walked with Tom to the center of the dance floor, and the tiny dog followed, wagging his tail. "How do we know what music to dance to if it's a silent rave?" she asked.

"Just sing a song in your head," said Tom.

"But won't we all run into each other?"

The main lights dimmed, and everyone around them began dancing. Tom tapped his feet awkwardly. Tink stood on his hind legs, looking unsure of himself. They were so self-conscious, she thought. A true heiress danced with no self-consciousness and without getting sweaty. She'd show them how.

Closing her eyes, she thought about the new song she was writing. It was edgier than her other music, the instruments more experimental, the lyrics more vulnerable. Too long and far-out and raw for a radio single. She hadn't told anyone about this song, not any of the men she was seeing, not even her producer or sister. For now, it was hers and hers alone because the only person she really wanted to hear the song was dead. It was a song about Gram, her very first best friend forever. Sometimes, Gram still visited her in dreams, her neck weighed down with heavy diamonds, her deep auburn hair flawlessly coiffed. "Do you know a psychic once told me you'd be one of the most photographed women in the world?" dream Gram would whisper into dream Paris's ear. "Never forget that you're a star."

After Gram's death, Paris had felt so lost and lonely. For weeks afterward, she'd find herself dialing Gram's phone number and then catch herself. On the day of the Beverly Hills funeral, when the paparazzi swarmed her walking out with the casket, blinding her already teary eyes with their flashes, Paris had nearly lashed out into the roar of clicking shutters, furious that they couldn't leave her alone with her grief and memories, not even on this one damn day. She'd lost so much. The one person who truly understood her and believed in her unequivocally. The song was about these memories and this loss. She hummed the melody to herself now, letting her arms and legs sway, no music video choreography to slow her down, no complicated dance steps to learn, no die-hard fans to impress or glittering cameras to seduce or carefully curated lifestyle products to sell. Like when she'd dated that male Paris but better because this was the Paris she'd wanted all along. Paris and Paris. Paris squared. Finally, she had time to think, to be alone with herself. Alone but not lonely.

Halfway through the song, she opened her eyes. Around her, the sailors and waitresses were bending and shaking, twisting and twirling, oblivious to their surroundings, lost in a private universe of individual rhythms. It was so different from her experiences DJing, conducting the crowd like an orchestra, setting the mood and pace. Here, they were all together in a sense, but she was not controlling them, nor they her. Everyone was free. Even Tom and Tinkerbell had loosened up. Tom was dancing the robot, his rigid arms bent at the elbows and scissoring through the air while Tink nipped at Tom's feet, his tail slapping the floor. Paris laughed, and Tom caught her staring. He blushed. When her song ended, he approached and offered his hand. "May I have this d-dance?"

Paris hesitated. What would Marilyn do? Surely Marilyn would never dance with someone so old, so broke, so aggressively unfashionable and possibly insane. *Someone might see.* But her fake tooth's ache like like like stopped her from saying no. A true heiress danced like no one was watching. Gram had taught her that. Now that she thought about it, even Marilyn had slipped up every now and then, marrying that dorky playwright and letting the press photograph her reading that lame Irish novel with the Greek name. It hadn't damaged Marilyn's brand *that* much, had it? Paris licked her lips, remembering Tom's earlier kindnesses. Was a dance really so much to ask?

She clasped his hand. They began dancing. She didn't even imagine a song this time, just let her feet glide across the floor with Tom's, the room silent except for the other tapping feet and the water rushing through the sewer pipes overhead. They danced fast songs and slow songs, the moonwalk and stanky leg. Despite her earlier reservations, she enjoyed herself. Tom was a surprisingly good dance partner. Graceful and energetic, quick on his toes. Between songs, she gazed into his moss-green eyes and wondered what he was thinking. Normally, guys only danced with her because they wanted something: sex, proximity, association.

Paris-sites, she dubbed them. But dancing with Tom was different. Like dancing with Gram, warm and innocent.

They were dancing a slow song now, her hands on his shoulders. He smiled at her—there were those horrible teeth—but she forced herself to look past them for now. Her tooth like like like tingled. He was not so bad looking for an old guy, she supposed. If you ignored the teeth, he had a nice smile. Kind and friendly. Behind the grizzled face and ugly buckteeth, she could see his true self now, the self that had drawn her in from the moment they first met. Someone waking after many years asleep. A younger, muscled man wearing a tiara over jet-black hair, pink glitter running through his veins. A man marching to the beat of his own clarinet. A man who let no one—not the dentist, not her—tell him who to be. A man who never let them break his heart. *Who never let them break his heart.* Now she knew what she'd noticed earlier but couldn't articulate: Tom was a true heiress. Poor, yes, but he had the inheritance, had always had it, would never abandon it. How had she not recognized this before?

After a few more songs, the rave ended. The strobe lights darkened, and the sailors shuffled back behind the bar. Tom's hand slid from Paris's back, leaving a cold dampness.

They agreed on a drink at the bar before going. "A pun for you," Tom said, after one of the many Beatrices had brought their drinks. "Why did the prawn leave the nightclub?" She shrugged, and he grinned, baring those horrible buckteeth. "Because he pulled a *mussel*. Get it?"

This time, she couldn't help it. She laughed. She laughed and laughed and didn't care who saw.

"I'm sorry we weren't able to find your friend," Tom said softly. "But I'm really glad you stayed here and danced with me." She blushed. "I haven't felt that free since..." He stared into his drink, biting his lip.

"I know what you mean," Paris said, thinking back to everything that had happened tonight, the tingling in her tooth that made her follow Tom through the sewer and then dance with him. "I feel different, too. Like I've been on this train for years and didn't know it, and mostly, I can't control the train, but there have been these brief moments tonight." She paused, and her tooth like like like tingled again. "These brief moments where I've felt I'm steering the train and switching it onto a new track, and in those moments, it's like time doesn't exist, and the laws of physics don't exist, and I can do whatever I want with that train. Paint it with pink glitter. Play my favorite K-pop, Drake, and Nicki Minaj songs. And I know I can't steer the train forever, but in those moments, it doesn't matter."

"The gap in Their conditioning," Tom muttered. "The break in continuity. The node. The 'like.'"

She smiled, not understanding. "Well, there's no sin in life worse than being boring."

"My dear, I wholeheartedly agree," said Tink, leaping from her lap to the counter. "Which is why we simply *must* get to the club to upstage one Kimberly Noel Kardashian West before your birthday magic disappears!"

The club. She was having so much fun she'd almost forgotten. The Beatrice who had brought their drinks now spun around, gaping at Tinkerbell. "Hon, did you say Kim Kardashian?"

Tink barked yes as Paris stared at Beatrice in shock, stomach plummeting. So these mole people had heard of Kim but not *her*? Beatrice pointed behind her to a small, muted television Paris hadn't noticed. On the screen, a smiling brunette was feeding a golden retriever dry dog food so totally not up to Tink's standards. "She was on the screen only a moment ago dancing somewhere in the West Village. Live episode of *Keeping Up with the Kardashians*. Just love that show, I do."

Beatrice handed Paris the remote. She turned up the volume, partly hoping Kim was not really on TV, that she could stay at the Sailor's Grave a little longer. Beside her, Tom reached into a small pistachio dish and cracked open a nut with his terrible teeth. He spat the shell into an empty dish, but she didn't recoil in disgust, as she would have earlier. He reached for another nut, brought the little notebook from his back pocket, and began scribbling away.

She peered over his shoulder and read a senseless word equation:

self ≥ hollowing out?

So it wasn't about her after all. Disappointing but not a huge loss. Those books in his apartment had looked super boring.

She returned to the TV. The dog food commercial ended, and the screen blackened. "Coming to Netflix," boomed the announcer, as Joaquin Phoenix's handsome face filled the screen, "*The Search for…*"

Tom seized the remote and flicked off the TV.

"What are you doing?" Paris asked, snatching at the remote as Tinkerbell growled. "We need to see where Kim is."

The color had drained from Tom's face. He was breathing hard and had spilled pistachio shells across the counter.
"The bartender is working for Them, a-and…"

So Tom was still a crazy old man. She'd seen ads everywhere for this upcoming Joaquin Phoenix Netflix special
about the missing writer, each more irritating than the last.
Why did people care so much about a boring writer, especially one who clearly didn't want to be found? They were
the same types who looked down on her as a ditzy, dumb
blonde without ever digging deeper. The same people who
gawked at Marilyn's funeral, pretending to care for the life
they'd consumed. Couldn't they see this highfalutin author
was building a brand, living off the grid just to generate
buzz and sell more books? When Tom stopped acting like
such a freak, she'd tell him about this show. Maybe he'd like
it, as a writer himself.

She wrestled the remote from Tom's trembling hands.
Defeated, he went back to eating the pistachios. She
turned the TV back on just in time to see Kim slipping into
an exclusive-looking club on Hudson Street.

"I know where that is," she announced, grabbing
Tom's arm with one hand and scooping up Tink with the
other. But when she looked up, Tom was holding a hand
to his mouth, wincing in pain. Her chest tightened.

"Here, let me see," she said softly, setting Tinkerbell back
on the barstool. Tom shook his head no, his face red, but she
told him it was OK, there was no reason to be ashamed. She
thought of Gram again. "Never forget that you're a star," she
told Tom. Slowly, he relented. She gently guided his hand

from his mouth and dropped it in his lap. He smiled weakly, and now she understood. It was his front right central incisor, his bucktooth, the part of himself he'd sworn never to change. He must have chipped it cracking open a pistachio. A tiny half-moon gap where once was smoothness.

*

When they finally emerged from the sewer, Tom pulled the lunch bag back over his head. Now that Paris's tooth was fixed, he hadn't asked her to wear one. She didn't care who saw her. The sun was lifting over the horizon, but the rain hadn't let up. The water splattered the brown paper. He wished he still had an umbrella. He worried the bag would fall apart, exposing him to an endless stream of fashionably drunk New Yorkers stumbling down Hudson Street like so many lost souls, so many pulsing electrons dissolving in his arms. Here was the last judgment parade of bearded men in tight pants and women wearing only black, assembled and taken apart, assembled and taken apart again, each with a vibrating phone, cordless earbuds, those little plastic cards in their wallets, the ebb and flow of information and capital, all those wires linking them to the grand conspiracy. Much as the outside world terrified him, he still needed this writing material. He'd also sworn to help Paris find the club and wouldn't leave until she was safely inside the Trystero. It was the least he could do after the night she'd shown him and the way she'd bucked him up after he chipped his tooth, telling him he was a "star."

He had no idea what that meant, but it made him feel better, if only momentarily. He'd been so upset about the tooth. After everything Eigenvalue had said earlier, he had no choice no choice no choice but to interpret the chipped tooth as a threat. A message from Them and Eigenvalue. Somehow, the dentist must have figured out Tom was going to the Sailor's Grave and asked the Beatrices to set out a bowl of pistachios. It was all so clear: Eigenvalue was hoping Tom would return to get his tooth fixed and then would alter his mind, his Tom-ness, pacifying him for easy delivery to Netflix. If that were the case though, if They'd already begun consuming him, why did he feel exactly the same?

past Tom 🦷 *future Tom???*

Maybe Mel was right. Maybe he was just paranoid for no reason. Hadn't Paris's new fake tooth allowed her to exercise greater free will, if only for brief moments? What she described with the train sounded so similar to the gaps in Their conditioning he'd theorized in *GR*.

Paris steers train = Valley girl "like" = gap in speech = 🦷 *= chance to deviate = node???*

As Paris led him down Hudson, her heels clicking on the drenched sidewalk, his thoughts drifted to the West Village of his youth. Years ago, he and Richard had hung out at the White Horse Tavern, nursing Red Cap ales and listening to Ornette Coleman. Ah, those were the days! Before he'd published *V.* and gone into hiding. Before Richard barreled across Carmel Valley at ninety miles per hour, flew from the red Harley like a fallen angel, wings clipped as he descended, descended, tearing through a barbed wire fence with a hellish fury and landing in a heap of fermenting vineyard grapes. A sickly transubstantiation: wine congealing to blood just two days after Richard's novel published. In a way, Richard had been the first to abandon him, the first to leave him all alone. Oh Richard, so perfect and free, so very, very dead.

> *Valley girl "like" / gap / freedom / node →*
> *Valley boy dead*

Tom was glad the old joint's white horse logo and neon sign had survived even as the surrounding street had transformed dramatically. Here was a new restaurant with a French-sounding name, a realty office with a crisp royal blue awning, a trendy sushi restaurant, and a Pure Barre studio. So he was not the only one who'd changed.

> *future Tom???*

In the end, you were always consumed no matter how hard you resisted. No choice no choice no choice. Shaking his head, he tried imagining what Richard would say if he were still alive. Richard the revolutionary. Richard the folk hero. He could almost see his friend on his Carmel cabin's porch plucking guitar strings and talking Castro, the wind teasing his curls and the sun tanning his muscled arms. Richard would almost certainly view Tom as a sellout and the Village as corrupted, but that was the thing about dying young. You never lived long enough to outgrow your own myths.

He licked his chipped tooth, trying to make peace with it, reminding himself of Paris's train and his nodes. Was it possible to be both free and commodified? Could an individual consciousness live on even as the body was consumed?

Tom – (consumed Tom) = who?

A few shops down from the White Horse Tavern, they arrived at their destination, a nondescript venue with a neon green Trystero horn over the door. A mountainous man in all black blocked the entrance. "Name?" he grunted, tapping his clipboard.

"You don't know who she is?" asked Tinkerbell.

The bouncer's face was still as stone. "Look, I got a lot of people wanting to get in here tonight. Just give me a name."

"I'm Paris," she said, her thin ankles splattered with mud. "You know, Paris the Heiress?"

The bouncer glanced at his clipboard and flipped to a new page. His eyes scanned from top to bottom, and then he peeled the page back. He was probably only eighteen or nineteen years old, too young to remember Paris's heyday. "Sorry, you're not here."

"But you don't understand," she pleaded, voice cracking. She glanced at Tom, her eyes begging him to back her up, but this was her Zone, her sewer. What could he do? "I'm Paris *Hilton*. Kim's in there, isn't she? I'm an old friend of Kim's. Kim was once my assistant, can you believe that?"

"You're not on the list," the bouncer growled. "The Trystero is members only."

"Well, if he thinks he's ever staying in a Hilton Hotel again, he's just *wrong*," snarled Tinkerbell.

Paris stared at her mud-splattered heels, her bottom lip quivering. "So we're not getting in after all," she told Tom. "I'm sorry for dragging you all this way…"

"Ith OK, really it ith," he said, only slightly embarrassed by his new lisp from the pistachio-chipped tooth. The club was stupid, her quest for fame was stupid, but he still felt bad for her. She'd had quite a night. He lifted an arm to pat her shoulder, but another arm—a younger man's arm in an ill-fitting, military-style jacket—pushed him away.

"Hey, it's OK, they're with me, and they're real groovy," said the arm's voice.

Tom turned and nearly fainted. It was Them! The voice belonged to none other than that actor, decked out in full Doc Sportello attire, right down to the sandals and hat. The others were here, too. Real Doc in his gold-tinted aviators, Lieutenant Tyrone Slothrop wearing dog tags and a crimson Harvard sweater, Oedipa Maas with her pile of Tupperware, and Herbert Stencil with his stack of journals, hair and clothes as rumpled as ever. Terrified as he was, Tom had to admit They looked well. All of Them! His lovely, lovely creations!

The bouncer waved them in, and he followed, holding on to his writing notebook for dear life. Inside, the music throbbed and pulsed, making his bones ache even as Paris brightened at his side, finally in her element. His eyes took a moment to adjust to the flashing purple lights, the blue-and-gold-tinted ceiling. On the dance floor, beautiful young people in shimmering metallic clothes glided back and forth, rubbing their sleek, warm bodies together

like well-oiled annihilation machines, tipping glowing drinks down their perfect plastic throats. At the bar,
a girl Jack's age poured shining, silver liquid into glasses,
her oily breasts spilling over a tight, black dress that appeared airbrushed onto her skin. Imagining particles colliding at the speed of light, his face flushed underneath the
bag. He pulled at the sides to let some air in, but the smells
of sex and sweat and fresh dollar bills were too intense.
He coughed, growing more paranoid by the second. What
if They figured out who he was? What if Paris gave him
away?

The actor directed them to a private table in the corner
with dark wine bottles. Tom squeezed into the booth between real Doc and Oedipa. Almost immediately, Oedipa
began pouring wine into her Tupperware containers, and
real Doc offered him a joint, which he refused. "Paris, Paris,
Paris!" the actor said, slapping his knees, clearly under the
influence of pot and maybe some heavier hallucinogens,
too. "This is groovy, really it is. I thought you and your
puppy were like, dead or something."

"Tink was, Joaquin, but not me," said Paris, so at ease she
was practically glowing. "I've just been behind the scenes
a little more, focusing on my company."

"It's Doc, actually," the actor winked. "Well anyway, good
to see you. Have you met my friends?" She shook her head,
and the actor went around the table, introducing them one
by one. Everyone waved politely at Paris, and Tom's chest
swelled with pride—such good manners he'd taught them!
"And your friend with the bag," the actor continued, turning now to Tom. "I don't think we've had the pleasure
of meeting."

The actor smiled, stretching the pink scar above his upper lip to a dangerous width: it was a miracle his face didn't tear in two. He held out his hand. "I'm Doc," he said, his bright green eyes searching through the holes of Tom's paper bag mask. Tom swallowed hard. He could feel the others watching, trying to figure him out. Stencil had stopped perusing his notebooks, and Slothrop was leering at him, fingering his silver dog tags. Tom curled his gnarled fingers around the actor's hand. The grip was firm and strong, the skin smooth and moist. The hand of a confident man. The hand of Them. One bounce, two bounce, three. "I'm T-tom," he gulped.

"*Paper Bag* Tom," said Doc. "It's a real groovy look, my friend. As I always say, change your hair, change your life."

The words split him open like an atom. He found it hard to breathe, his heart ripped by thousands of explosions. That was *his* line. He'd thought it. He'd written it as dialogue for Doc in *Inherent Vice*. Now the words were no longer his but *Theirs*. They'd turned not only his own characters but his own words—the materials from which he had formed Them all and formed himself—against him.

He could feel Them reaching in and rewiring his circuits, holding his individual consciousness between thumb and forefinger, toying with him before They snuffed it out. For fifty years, he had walled himself off from the life he so loved, losing friendships and sleep, missing jazz concerts and soccer games and birthdays, and always taking precautions, always looking over his shoulder, always staying one step ahead. He had put himself through hell, put Mel and Jack through hell, and for what? None of it had even mattered. He could see that now, clear as day.

He looked around at his lovely creations and felt an immense sadness, vast as the ocean and deep as the void. Like Eigenvalue, They'd all sold themselves to the dark side. Soon his other characters would too, and They'd sell him to Netflix to boot. He thought of all those parents on TV with downcast eyes and stuttering lips whose kids had grown up to become serial rapists, serial killers, domestic terrorists, IBM employees, Eisenhower Republicans. No, no, no, he would *not* be one of them. He would not let his creations destroy his life. He would not be Their victim. They could not take anything else from him, not one single word more. But how? With the tip of his tongue, he like like like tapped his newly chipped tooth's jagged edge. His chest tightened, and he suddenly knew what he had to do.

Give up writing.

It was all so obvious now. Who needed the Pulitzer or Nobel's approval? Roth had retired at seventy-nine, Munro at eighty-one, and now it was his time. He would abandon his anonymity and rejoin the world. All along, he'd thought Paris was the detective on a doomed quest or that They were the detectives searching for him, the grail. Now he understood: *he* was the detective, the book was the grail, and writing was the doomed quest. For years, he'd thought abandoning writing would mean abandoning himself, but it was the opposite. In continuing to write, he'd allowed Them to dictate everything about his life. But he didn't have to continue this journey of perpetual deferment, did he? No, he had a *choice* here. He wouldn't allow Them to imprison him in his own home any longer. He'd stop providing Them with the locks and bars, his words. Nor would he ever write about Paris. He wouldn't betray her like that, wouldn't allow Them to twist her fictional depiction into whatever They felt like, wouldn't destroy her Paris-ness. The thing he couldn't describe or quantify, the thing that differentiated her from the other hundred billion who'd walked this earth. To think he was going to write about her! He was no better than those producers on her first show! No better than Blicero sacrificing a human life to launch his Rocket!

> *writing greatest book ever ≠ one single human life!!!*

> *bureaucrat-engineer / TV producer / paparazzi ≥ author!!!*

A lump lodged in his throat. His stomach twisted into knots, and he thought he might retch. But he could fix it. He *would* fix it. He'd throw away the notebook. Mend his marriage and his relationship with his son. This was the last part of himself They couldn't take. This was the gap. The node. The brief moment where he steered the train before it was taken from him. He stood up, his hands trembling, his tooth like like like tingling, and he was still himself, still Thomas Pynchon. "It wath nithe meeting you all, but I have t-to get going now. I'm not feeling well and thould get home."

"What do you mean you're leaving?" Paris gasped. "We haven't even *seen* Kim yet."

He sighed. She deserved some explanation after all they'd been through together. He guided her to a nearby table out of earshot.

"It's 'Them' again, isn't it?" she asked, using air quotes. "They're here?"

"They are. They a-are very much here. You underthtand, don't you? In the thame way you couldn't be theen with your knocked out tooth, ith hard for me to be around Them. I jutht need thome freth air ith all, need to get home to my family."

Paris nodded slowly, glancing at her feet. "I understand," she said. "It's just, I didn't realize you'd leave so soon. Will we ever see each other again?"

His mouth went dry. Of course they'd never see each other again. She could never know his true identity, and the realization filled him with despair. He would miss the way he felt around her, so accepted and understood, would miss her the way he still missed Richard. He thought of the little girl who wanted to be a veterinarian. They were not so different, he now realized. Hiding all these years with his words, he'd also lost part of himself. He and Paris had fought the same enemy with different weapons—he with retreat, she with submersion—each aspiring to remain true to the self in a world that undermined the self at every turn. A losing battle, all things considered. Surely, she could handle one more lie.

"Of courthe," he said. "I'm going to need a few more quoteth. For the magathine profile, a really flattering piethe." Paris smiled. He gazed into her eyes, at the sliver of brown iris peaking from behind her blue contact lens. Her Paris-ness. He recalled the Von Braun epigraph he'd used in the first part of *GR*: "Nature does not know extinction; all it knows is transformation." He'd meant the quote to refer to a conditioned response's lack of total extinction, but now he saw it referred to the persistence of the unconditioned self, too.

> *Paris – (conditioned Paris) =* ~~*who?*~~
> *private griefs + veterinarian dreams + caring friend + dancing like no one's watching = unconditioned Paris = brown iris =*
> *PARIS*

> ~~*self ≥ hollowing out?*~~

> *self > hollowing out!!!!*

Paris blinked, and the brown disappeared again, hidden but not gone. "Of courthe we'll thee each other again. I'll be in touch."

Outside, the sun had finally risen, bathing the street in a gentle, orange glow. He took a deep breath. His nausea had disappeared. The air drifting through the paper bag's holes smelled like the old days. Sour fermented piss and Marlboro cigarettes, salt-drenched French fries. He bent over, resting his hands on his knees, his programmed heart pounding, the rain beating down as he listened to the sounds of early morning Manhattan. A yellow cab slithering down the drenched streets, a suited businesswoman ordering coffee and bagel from a cart, a bearded shopkeeper unfurling his storefront's steel gate with a rolling clatter. The whole night had been full of close calls—none closer than this—but at last he was headed home to those he loved.

He straightened out and began the short walk back to the sewer, his limbs sore and his face chafing from the soaked paper bag, devastation melting to relief. Staying out all night at his age on a fool's errand—who would have thought? He shook his head.

Soon, ordinary New Yorkers would rise for work. Any minute now, Mel's alarm clock would sound, and she'd wonder where he was. He knew her morning routine by heart: two cups of dark roast, a light gray pantsuit, papers crammed into an overflowing black leather purse. Every morning, he'd walked her to the elevator, kissed her goodbye, and then returned to their spacious apartment alone. Every morning, he'd returned to the indecipherable black scribbles on blue graph paper and the soiled paperbacks with broken spines and the whispering fears and the black burning paranoia and the words, words, nothing but words to keep him company all day, nothing but words to wall him off from Them but not from himself until at last, Mel returned home in the evening.

$$(words + words) \, \hat{} \, words \times (words \times words \times words \times words) + words + WORDS = ?????$$

But no more. For the first time in years, he didn't have writer's block. He knew exactly which words to use: *I'm sorry. I'm sorry for hurting you both. I'm sorry for not being there for you and not putting our family first. I'm sorry I'm sorry I'm sorry. I love you, and never forget that you're stars. That you're my stars.*

He would tell Mel and Jack as soon as he got home. No more writing. No more anonymity. No more putting anything ahead of his family. For now, he could think of nothing more appropriate than to quote Didion. "Goodbye to all that," he whispered. And then he yelled it at the top of his lungs, startling the businesswoman across the street, "Goodbye! Goodbye! Goodbye!"

He began singing:

> Too many chain-link fenceth in the evening,
> Too many people thivering in the rain,
> They tell me that you finally got around to have your baby,
> And it don't look like I'll thee your fathe again.
> Thometimeth I wanna go back north, to Humboldt County—
> Thometimeth I think I'll go back eatht, to thee my kin...
> There'th timeth I think I almotht could be happy
> If I knew you thought about me, now and then...

At the sewer, he paused. Dug his worn sneakers into the pavement. Tore his notebook into the tiniest of shreds. The rain had eased up, but the paper bag still clung to his skin. He ripped it off. Stood in the sacred, orange light of the mechanical new day, not caring who saw or who might snap his picture, letting the wind tickle his cheeks and the rain soak his clothes. What Paris had taught him was this: He'd been wrong about freedom. Freedom wasn't locking yourself in the house. It wasn't sealing yourself off in a time capsule with delusions of escaping corruption and remaining pure. It was *this*. Choosing not to betray your friends and loved ones. Feeling the sun on your skin and countless other mindless pleasures. Dancing with abandon in the middle of the night. Finding peace in your city and peace with your-self. Ah, this was nice. This was really something special, this was the one freedom and salvation, and no one—not even Them and not even Their God—could take it away.

*

Joaquin was grinning when Paris returned to their table at the Trystero. "I hope you don't mind, but we've been joined by a few others," he said, showing off his artificially tobacco-stained teeth. He gestured behind him, where a film crew was setting up. "It's part of the reality show. I'm sure you've heard of it by now?" She nodded, faking a smile. "And of course, our good friend, Ian Scuffling, a former war correspondent who's been writing some ar-ticles about us." He pointed at Slothrop, who was jotting down notes on a steno pad and now looked nothing like the college boy lieutenant she'd first seen. A real downgrade in the fashion department. He'd exchanged his sweater and dog tags for a horribly rumpled button-down and the same wire-rim glasses that look terrible on everyone.

"So we're going to be on TV," Paris said, trying to steady her voice so they wouldn't sense her excitement. "Like, right now?"

Joaquin nodded. "In a few minutes. Maybe you can help us actually. We're looking for a reclusive author."

"Oh, Joaquin, stop wasting your time," called a low, creaking voice Paris would recognize anywhere. "It's not like Paris has time to read, you know?"

Paris turned around, her heart sliding into her stom-ach. For weeks, she'd imagined this meeting with Kim. Her birthday magic, she was sure, would lend her a special glow, like a pregnant woman, that little extra something Gram always had and that would make everyone look at *her* and not at Kim, who would have a terrible hair day or a bad pimple. Now she realized this was only wishful thinking. Kim looked *stunning*. Like always. Tonight, her former assistant was wearing a sparkly black mini with black ankle booties, her hair piled high in a faux mohawk, half-up and half-down do, skin glowing, eyes perfectly kohled.

"I mean, Paris must be so *busy* these days," Kim continued over Tinkerbell's growls. "That must be why she's disappeared from TV and has so few Insta followers. She's like, a respectable *businesswoman* these days, isn't that right, Paris?"

"I have been out of the public eye a little," she admitted, unable to meet Kim's eyes.

"I'm surprised Paris even made it out tonight," Kim continued. "Why don't you let Paris get home to her spreadsheets or whatever? Come to the VIP room with me and my sisters, let us improve your ratings."

Paris sunk into her chair. Next time, if there were a next time, Kim should just bitch-slap her in the face. There was no greater sin than being boring and unworthy of attention, no bigger humiliation than getting called boring right to your face. In front of a hot guy no less! She turned now to Joaquin. His face reddened, and his bushy sideburns twitched. So maybe he wasn't actually *that* hot, but he was hottish, had understood the diss, and was embarrassed for her, maybe even pitied her, which she couldn't bear. Joaquin stared into his drink, took a long sip, and stood up.

"Sorry, Paris, I know it's anti-groovy and all for me to leave, but she's right. I need Kim to make a cameo appearance on the show to help with our ratings. But before I go, I want to show you a picture of the author. Just in case." He pulled a crumpled flyer from his trendily vintage army coat's breast pocket. "Here's an old picture from his college days, one of the only pictures we have actually. A major bummer. Dude should be in his late seventies, early eighties now. His last name's Pynchon."

She glanced at the flyer in Joaquin's hands. In all the ads and commercials she'd seen for the show, she had yet to see a photo of the author, and now she understood why: the author *badly* needed a makeover. Unfortunately, there wasn't much to work with. His dark hair was stupidly brushed up in the front above thick eyebrows, lopsided eyes, and enormous ears. From there, it only got worse. Half-smiling and half-smirking, his lips bared some of the worst, snaggliest buckteeth she'd ever seen. *Literally the absolute worst.* She let out a little involuntary gasp.

"What did you say his first name was?"

"Thomas. Thomas Pynchon."

Her mouth fell open.

"What? What is it? Have you seen him?" asked Joaquin, unable to hide his excitement. He stepped closer, and she breathed in Doc's carefully crafted scent, a mixture of top tier marijuana, frozen pizza, and old sneakers.

The film crew moved in closer, fingers poised over the record buttons. Scuffling whipped out his notebook and began writing furiously. She knew she had two choices here: She could betray Tom and revive her career, or she could remain silent and true to their friendship. She knew what the hot thing to do was, knew what Joaquin wanted her to do, knew what Marilyn and Kim and the old Paris would have done given the same circumstances. But maybe there was a new way to be hot. Maybe being hot was just being a good friend. Maybe she didn't need fame to escape loneliness. She just needed herself and a few people who cared about her. Her tooth like like like tingled. Tinkerbell purred in her arms, his little body quivering with excitement. She looked from one expectant face to the next, the tingling in her tooth growing worse, and then she looked inside, deep inside, past the baby voice and the pink Bentley, the fake eyelashes and the Mystic Tan, the bejeweled cell phone, the paparazzi pose, the Ugg boots and sparkly stilettos, the frenemy fights over stolen boyfriends, the catchphrase and the sex tape and even the entourage of little dogs, purebred kittens, mini pigs, ferrets, and exotic kinkajou monkeys, past all of that, past the nightmares that left her shaking, the betrayals and abuse, all those invisible scars and long-buried traumas and the ways she had fought to conceal them and protect herself, past all of that too, deep inside, her tooth like like like like like like LIKE practically on fire now, to the part of herself she hadn't sold and never would. It was there. They had never taken it from her. The inheritance of all true heiresses. This time, she asked herself a new question. WWPD: What would Paris do?

Rule number twenty-one: *Never be predictable.*

"Sorry, I haven't seen him. I don't know who you're talking about."

She was steering the train now, flying down the tracks, everything a pink blur, and then like like like like like like like like it was gone. The film crew stopped filming, Scuffling stopped writing, and Joaquin's smile faded.

"Well, that's too bad, Paris. That's really too bad." He returned the flyer to his breast pocket and motioned for the film crew to follow him into the back room. Before they left, Kim turned around and shot Paris one last duck face of pure loathing and triumph that Paris would never forget: those raised eyebrows so perfectly arched and gelled with Anastasia Beverly Hills products, those pursed pouting lips in just the right shade of Christian Louboutin!

"You're going to let them go? Just like that?" said Tinkerbell. The little Chihuahua was sitting on the arm of her chair, his oversize ears pricked, his eyes dark and slick as caviar. When she didn't answer, he hopped down and pointed a paw toward Joaquin's film crew. "I hope you can understand," he said, twisting his head to stare at her over his sweatered shoulder. "But I don't need *you* to be famous, my dear. I'm a talking dog after all."

The betrayal hit her hard. It was worse than her parents sending her to the hell school, worse even than Rick publishing the sex tape. She lunged, wrapping her body around the dog's sleek, shuddering frame. "Tink, you don't have to do this. Tink, you *can't* do this. You're my best friend in the world!" But all the tenderness was gone. Tink's true inner heiress was dead. Snarling and yelping, clawing at Paris's skin with his perfectly manicured nails, Tinkerbell sunk his freshly brushed teeth into the flesh of her forearm. She cried out. Her grip loosened, and the dog slid from her arms. Her last view was of his little tan tail, held straight and high like a Gucci umbrella stem, weaving back and forth through the crowd of dress shoes. Then he was gone. After his fame just like the rest. That wasn't hot, it wasn't hot at all.

Crouching on the dirty dance floor, she hugged her knees to her chest and rocked back and forth while the other club-goers carried on around her. Like they couldn't even see her. Like she was locked in the cinder-block chamber again and didn't even exist. But she *did*, she reminded herself. She did exist. She had marched out of that place with her head held high and would do the same here. *Come on, Paris. You can do this.* She closed her eyes and felt the tickle of Gram's warm breath in her ear, the soft embrace of her gentle whisper, and wasn't this the only kind of grace she needed? Not a divine grace but a human grace, another person's unconditional acceptance and love. *Never forget that you're a star.* She would tell this to Lily later, when she visited them all, Nicky and James and Lily, and she thought again of the voicemail from earlier, her darling little Lily singing her happy birthday, and the wonderful night she'd just spent with her new friend Tom, the basic kindness in his eyes. For the final time that night, Paris pulled herself to her feet, dusted off her dress, and adjusted her tiara. She had people who loved her. Why had it taken her so long to realize nothing else mattered? A true heiress never lets her heart get broken, she reminded herself. No, a true heiress is the one breaking hearts.

*

The Heiress steps outside, shielding her eyes from the blistering sunrise. Even without her magic, it's still her birthday, bitchessss. In the distance, she sees the Author. A solitary figure silhouetted against the slate gray city. A stooped-over cutout wearing ill-fitting clothes and needing a shave. How many just like him has she passed without a second glance? The Author is holding the paper bag in one hand, eyes squeezed shut, grizzled head thrown back to greet the last few rain drops. The rainbow is raging across the sky now, that candy-colored arc slicing through this city of steel-eyed solitude and cement-cased dreams. The Heiress remembers it in her bones and in her new tooth. That angered ache and paralyzing pull of gravity beyond the zero, the movement from death to death-transfigured. It is unlike before. Unlike anything she's ever felt: throat numbing and chest melting and heart emptying out like the last subway car at the final stop, every greased plastic seat wiped clean and glitter bombed. The rusted wrought iron streetlights are drunken It Girl angels slumping toward her and the glassy skyscrapers are trembling and the seams of her dress unthreading. A bulletproof window shatters to her left. A blackened brick falls inches from her perfectly pedicured toes. Glass particles sear her nostrils and glitter her hair as diamonds dive from her earlobes, pooling at her feet. Her necklace's incandescent orbs plunge like round, little hail lumps to the ash-stained pavement. She can hear it already, the rumbling of a deep and relentless hunger and the hellish screams of a million hoarse throats. All around her, true heiresses. All around her, the last judgment smells of burning plastic and slow-simmered trash and singed human flesh trapped in the frequencies.

"Tom," the Heiress calls out.

The Author opens his eyes, lifts his head, and turns toward the sound. Electric sparks dance through his mustache like tinsel on a Christmas tree. He doesn't feel a thing. He's playing bass guitar with his son in Brooklyn or strolling along the Hudson River with his wife. He's at the node, living between the wars and the frames and the opening and closing lines of the novel, riding the Valley girl "like," free for just this millisecond out of time, fragmenting like Slothrop and dissolving into the universe. "Yeth?"

Will you be my new best friend? Even after saying it so many times, the words catch in the Heiress's throat.

The Author can't hear the Heiress over the noise, but he understands. They're both just weirdos on each other's wavelengths now, fusing into one consciousness outside history's flow, all their past betrayals like like like like like like like like like like forgiven. He is smiling. His teeth are falling out one by one. The rockets are dismantling, the film running backward. The rain-soaked pavement is melting under their feet, and they're both sinking away from it all, the positive and the negative, the zero and the one, the tabloid cover girls and Paris-sitic paparazzi. The sky is heating up now, slate gray vaporizing into neon orange and electric violet and the hottest of hot pinks. The water has bubbled over the sides of the coal-black tea kettle, and the alarms are blazing. They will not cover their scarred ears or smear ash from their burning eyes or pick small rocks from the holes in their stained clothes. They will not hear the explosion before it hits.

Their eyes meet. The Author and the Heiress both blink once. Now everybody—

***

Author's Note

The stories in this collection are works of fiction. They should not be read as journalism, biography, history, or as truthful, accurate, objectively factual depictions of individuals, places, events, or other entities. Any references to historical events, real people, real places, or other real entities are used fictitiously and for the purposes of artistic expression and storytelling.

Nonetheless, these fictional stories do draw upon reported details, and I would like to acknowledge the following source materials, which I have creatively shaped and subjectively interpreted to express my own artistic vision.

*

"Alternative Facts" is a work of fiction that draws upon reported details about Kellyanne Conway's life and references an alleged punching incident that was widely reported and traced back to a known eyewitness, journalist Charles Gasparino. My story uses fiction to imagine the circumstances and the character's innermost thoughts leading up to this alleged incident. In this speculative endeavor, I drew upon Jarret Berenstein's *The Kellyanne Conway Technique* (2017) and a *New York Daily News* article by Chris Sommerfeldt ("Trump Advisor Kellyanne

Conway Allegedly Punched a Man in the Face at President Trump's Inaugural Ball," Jan. 24, 2017).

*

"Black Box" is a work of fiction, not biography. It draws upon many biographical details and incidents from B. F. Skinner's life, but I have also invented others and taken numerous poetic liberties to bring the story alive emotionally and dramatically. The dictionary definitions that appear at the beginning of my story are (in order) from *Merriam-Webster's Dictionary*, adapted from Wikimedia Commons and various popular news sources, adapted from the *Fontana Dictionary of Modern Thought*, and adapted from the *Internet Encyclopedia of Philosophy* and the *Stanford Encyclopedia of Philosophy*. The story includes quotes from B. F. Skinner's "Pigeons in a Pelican" (*American Psychologist*, 1960), *The Shaping of a Behaviorist* (1979), and *Walden Two* (1948). I was inspired to structure the story as a series of boxes after reading Daniel W. Bjork's *B. F. Skinner: A Life* (1993), which I also consulted for biographical details. In addition to Bjork's biography, I also drew upon James H. Capshew's "Engineering Behavior: Project Pigeon, World War II, and the Conditioning of B. F. Skinner" (*Technology and Culture*, 1991).

*

"Houston, We've Had a Problem" is a work of fiction that quotes dialogue from the following films: *Apocalypse Now* (1979), *Apollo 13* (1995), *Casablanca* (1942), *Goldfinger* (1964), *Gone with the Wind* (1939), *Good Morning, Vietnam* (1987), *Groundhog Day* (1993), *The Dark Knight* (2008), *The Silence of the Lambs* (1991), *A Streetcar Named Desire* (1951), *Taxi Driver* (1976), *Titanic* (1997), and *The Wizard of Oz* (1939).

*

"Lost in the Desert of the Real" is a work of fiction that draws upon numerous journalistic accounts, including published firsthand eyewitness testimonies, government documents, television reports and interviews, and publicly shared social media posts and videos about the false missile alert that occurred in Hawaii on January 13, 2018. However, I moved beyond the established facts of this event and included fictional, fantastical, exaggerated elements.

The real, the fake, the historical, and the fictional are deliberately confused. Events are compressed and combined. With the exception of the public figures used fictitiously, individuals who appear in the source materials have been anonymized, disguised, merged with other individuals, or combined with totally invented characters; all other characters are wholly my invention, and their resemblance to actual persons, living or dead, is entirely coincidental.

The story's epigraph is from Jean Baudrillard's *Simulacra and Simulation* (1981). I also include tweets from @realDonaldTrump and @JimCarrey that were posted on January 13, 2018. The story references scenes and characters from *The Truman Show* (1998), for the purpose of making original commentary.

*

"Tonight Show" is a work of fiction that includes several lines of dialogue and a description of George W. Bush and Jay Leno's interaction on an episode of *The Tonight Show* that aired November 19, 2013. The scenes from George W.

Bush's childhood draw upon widely reported details about the Bush family, but the situations, interactions, actions, inner thoughts, character motivations, and dialogue are all my invention. My research for this story draws upon George W. Bush's *Decision Points* (2010) and Elizabeth Mitchell's *W: Revenge of the Bush Dynasty* (2000).

*

"From the Eyes of Travelers" is a work of fiction that draws upon reported details about the 2016 assassination of Russian ambassador Andrei Karlov, the assassin Mevlüt Mert Altıntaş, and the Associated Press photojournalist Burhan Ozbilici. Karlov, Altıntaş, and Ozbilici are used fictitiously; all other characters are my invention, and their resemblance to other people, living or dead, is coincidental. The story references Ozbilici's photo series *An Assassination in Turkey* (2016); photographs from this series were widely published in newspapers.

To build my fictitious character Oz, I drew upon details from Ozbilici's first-person written account published by AP ("Witness to an Assassination," Dec. 19, 2016), Brian Horton's *Associated Press Guide to Photojournalism* (2000), and other journalistic articles. Everything else about the characters is purely my invention.

*

"The Author and the Heiress" is a work of fiction that draws upon reported details about Paris Hilton, Thomas Pynchon, and their associates while inventing numerous others. The incidents, situations, interactions, inner thoughts, character motivations, and dialogue in my story are all invented, except where noted below. All references to real people, places, and other entities are used fictitiously. The story also draws upon and references characters, settings, and concepts from Thomas Pynchon's novels that I have adapted, remixed, transformed, exaggerated, parodied, dramatized, and reimagined.

Paris Hilton has alleged publicly that she suffered abuse at several boarding schools she attended as a teenager. My story references similar alleged incidents in a fictitious manner and merges them into a single fictional, unnamed school.

The story includes quotes from Paris Hilton's *Confessions of an Heiress* (2004). Some of the anecdotes and explanations from this book also work their way into the character's thoughts and dialogue. The character Paris Hilton sometimes speaks or thinks lines that the real-life Paris Hilton has actually said. The story's first two sentences and last partial sentence, which also appear in one additional scene, are from Thomas Pynchon's *Gravity's Rainbow* (1973), as are the two songs that the Tom character sings to the Paris character; the second song was altered to accommodate the character's lisp. The quote by Arthur Salm appeared in a February 8, 2004 article in the *San Diego-Union Tribune* ("A Screaming Comes across the Sky [but Not a Photo]").

Of the many books, articles, and documentaries consulted, the following were especially useful: *The Cambridge Companion to Thomas Pynchon* (2011) by Inger H. Dalsgaard, et al.; *This Is Paris* (2020), directed by Alexandra Dean; *Thomas Pynchon: A Journey into the Mind of P.* (2002), directed by Fosco and Donatello Dubini; *Paris Hilton: A*

Biography (2011) by Sandra Gurvis; *Confessions of an Heiress* (2004) and *Paris: The Memoir* (2023) by Paris Hilton; *Paris, Not France* (2008), directed by Adria Petty; *Slow Learner* (1984) by Thomas Pynchon; "Meet Your Neighbor, Thomas Pynchon" by Nancy Jo Sales (*New York* magazine, Nov. 11, 1996); "Thomas Pynchon Returns to New York, Where He's Always Been" by J. K. Trotter (*The Atlantic*, Jun. 17, 2013); and *A Gravity's Rainbow Companion: Sources and Contexts for Pynchon's Novel* (1998) by Steven Weisenburger.

Acknowledgments

I am so grateful to the entire staff and board of Kallisto Gaia Press for bringing *Alternative Facts* into the world with a special thank you to Tony Burnett for his patience and guidance at every step. Without small presses like Kallisto Gaia that champion storytelling over the bottom line, a book like this would never have seen the light of day. Thank you also to the 2023 Acacia Fiction Prize judge, Lesley Bannatyne, for believing in my manuscript.

I was fortunate to work with wonderful editors and designers on this book. Jack Livings helped me push each story to its fullest potential, Christopher Santantasio gave me incredibly helpful feedback on "The Author and the Heiress" at a crucial time, Maria Eliades helped me with the cultural and linguistic details in "From the Eyes of Travelers," and Jennie Cohen did a superb copyedit. Thank you also to Raúl Lázaro for designing the perfect cover—I love it!

Thank you to the following journals and editors for giving these stories their first homes and edits: Matilda Bathurst of the *Iowa Review*; Adam Berlin and Jeffrey Heiman of *J Journal*; Jason Lee Brown, Michael Martone, and Shanie Latham of *New Stories from the Midwest*; Matt Coz of *Greensboro Review*; Elizabeth McKenzie of *Chicago*

Quarterly Review; Mark Nowak, Polly Rosenwaike, Aaron Stone, and H.R. Webster of *Michigan Quarterly Review*; and Andrew Tonkovich of *Santa Monica Review*. Thank you for supporting emerging writers.

Over the years, I have been fortunate to study writing with amazing teachers. Thank you to Joanie Mackowski, Stephanie Vaughn, and Helena Viramontes for teaching me to write fiction. My very first fiction class at Cornell was with Michael Koch, who was hugely influential and is dearly missed. Michael was the first person to tell me that I was already a writer: "A writer is just someone who writes." Thank you also to Michelle Caplan for teaching me much of what I know about writing and publishing. Many of these stories were first workshopped during my MFA program at Ohio State, and I am forever indebted to the prose faculty for nurturing my development as a writer: Lee Martin, Angus Fletcher, Elissa Washuta, and Nick White. This book would never have been possible without my thesis advisor, Michelle Herman, who has taught me so much not only about writing but life. I am so grateful for Michelle's continued friendship and mentorship.

Besides my teachers, I am also incredibly grateful to members of the Greenpoint Writers Core Group for their feedback and for showing me what a true literary community looks like: Emma Brodie, Nicholas DiMichele, Isabella Esser-Munera, Jonathan Herzog, Crispin Kott, Nathaniel Kressen, Logan Medland, Heather Newberger, Luke Ohlson, Danielle Pollack, Abby Ronner, Vinny Senguttuvan, and Laura Weinert-Kendt. I would never have been able to revise these stories without in-depth feedback from the three fiction cohorts that overlapped mine at Ohio State. It was a true gift workshopping with such talented writers and careful readers: Alaina Belisle, Liz Blackford, Scott Broker, Sheldon Costa, Kris Edwards, Mohan Fitzgerald, Morgan Fox, Neil Grayson, Adam Luhta, Krishna Mishra, Molly Rideout, and Margie Sarsfield. Special thanks to Molly Brown, Meagan McAlister, and Christopher Santantasio for being the very best writer friends and sounding boards throughout my book's journey to publication. Thank you also to Mark Mangelsdorf for being the best writer pen pal and a great reader.

As a new author, I had many questions. Karin Cecile Davidson, Erika Dreifus, Anne Jones, and Rebecca Turkewitz provided excellent advice about being a debut small press author and were unbelievably generous with their time. Thank you also to Darryl Jennings, Andrew Kagen, Melanie Katzman, and Sharon Makowsky for answering my legal and book launch questions. I am so lucky to have a terrific sister-in-law, Fern Diaz, who also happens to be a marketing genius and helped me with absolutely everything. My manuscript would never have realized its full potential as a book without Fern's expertise, enthusiasm, decisiveness, and creativity.

My family has supported me at every step. Thank you Mom, Dad, Sara, Jacob, Adam, Mimi, Valerie, Rick, Matt, Fern, Melissa, Kurt, and my entire extended family for your love, advice, and cheerleading. My late grandfather taught me to love reading and learning, and I feel his warmth and wisdom with me as I write. Lastly, thank you to my amazing partner, Andrew, who supports, encourages, challenges, and inspires me every day. I could never have written these stories without you.

About the Author

Emily Greenberg was born and raised in Memphis, Tennessee. She graduated from Cornell University and holds an MFA from the Ohio State University, where she was a Distinguished University Fellow. Her short fiction and essays have appeared in the *Iowa Review, Michigan Quarterly Review, Witness, Big Fiction, Santa Monica Review, Chicago Quarterly Review*, the tenth anniversary edition of *New Stories from the Midwest*, and elsewhere. Her writing honors include the Witness Literary Award in Fiction and two Pushcart Prize Special Mentions. She has taught at the Ohio State University, Columbus College of Art & Design, and the University of California in San Diego, where she currently lives with her husband. *Alternative Facts* is her first book and was named a runner-up for the Acacia Fiction Prize and BOA Editions Short Fiction Prize. Learn more at emilygreenberg.net.